SCARED STIFF

SCARED STIFF

The Old Swamp Road and other scary
stories to help you become scared stiff

To Tammi Giglio,
   I hope you and your
students enjoy my stories
but don't get too scared.

Charles Young

Written and Illustrated by
Charles Young

To order additional copies of this book, contact:
Xlibris Corporation
1-888-795-4274
www.Xlibris.com
Orders@Xlibris.com
71511

CONTENTS

Dear students, parents, and teachers,

Most of the stories in this book include elements of both fantasy and reality. Being able to tell the difference is an important reading skill that will be helpful throughout your school career and beyond. In writing these stories I used many experiences from my childhood and also from my thirty-five year teaching career.

My experiences provided the reality part of these stories. But my life was not quite a bizarre as some of these tales, so I had to use my imagination to come up with the fantasy or horror fiction parts. Fantasy can help make the stories become scary and interesting, but these things did not really happen to me . . . and I'm glad about that. Read these "reality horror" stories for the thrill and pleasure of the adventure, but try not to become "scared stiff."

Fantasy—uses magic and supernatural forms as a primary element of the plot, theme, and/or setting. It usually has make-believe creatures and exotic fantasy worlds. Many times it is based in the medieval period or uses medieval references and characters. It is fiction writing.

Horror fiction—is intended to scare, unsettle, or horrify the audience. It got its beginnings in 1764 and gained popularity in 1818 with Mary Shelley's story of Frankenstein. Frankenstein also has elements of science fiction.

Science fiction—often involves speculations based on current or future science or technology. The setting may be contrary to known reality. Science fiction may include: outer space, aliens, robots, and faster-than-light travel.

Reality horror—adds supernatural elements into everyday human experiences. They started calling it this in the 1960's. It is exceptionally suspenseful or frightening.

Charles Young, Author

ACKNOWLEDGEMENTS

There are so many people who have supported me in my efforts to write this book. I especially want to thank my wife, Gail, who listened patiently as I read her my rough drafts. Her honest suggestions and ideas were invaluable. My daughters, Sherri, Kathi, and Natali have given me numerous suggestions for story ideas or editorial changes.

Natali, a fifth grade teacher, and Kathi, a fourth grade teacher, have given me feedback from their students after reading many of these stories to them.

Another audience that has been very helpful and supportive is my grandchildren: Alexis, Nick, Michael, Zack, and Caden. They have listened lovingly to my stories and encouraged me to write more of them.

I also want to thank my parents for providing me with so many opportunities when I was a kid to explore the outdoors and use my imagination. Many of these stories reflect these adventures.

I would like to thank my friend, Lou Brooks, who I corroborated with as a kid in writing and drawing many comic strips. Now, with his vast experience as a professional artist, he has given me many suggestions on how to get started in the book publishing process.

Several of my stories are about things that happened during my 35 years of teaching and I would like to thank all my students and fellow teachers for the story concepts they provided. Teaching is a very rewarding career, and I want to continue to entertain and teach students through my books.

Charles Young

The Old Swamp Road

The boys and I love to explore the woods and hills around our small town. But, there is one place that we are still a little afraid to venture into . . . and that is the swampy area to the south of town. There still is an old dirt road that goes through the swamp, but it hasn't been traveled on in years. After all the trouble with the road in the past, it was decided to build a new paved road into town that went around the swampland rather than right through the middle of it. Over the years, people have claimed to see some sort of swamp creature roaming in the swamp. The legends about this creature grew to such proportions that the road was finally closed.

In case you want to know, I'm Stevie and I'm currently in the fifth grade at Morton Elementary School in Littleneck, Louisiana. My classmates and good buddies, Gil and Robbie, can't wait till school is out so we all can go on our little adventures before it starts getting dark. We all hurry home and get our schoolwork done. This is one of our family rules. Then we head for the hills. We all know that we must be home for dinner on time (another rule) or else we will be grounded for a week.

We had so many good times that I can't remember them all. But after a month or so we were getting a little bored by going to the same places and decided we needed to try something new. We sat around and thought about it, but nothing was jumping right out at us. Finally, Gil (which is short for Gilbert, but only his mother calls him that when she is angry at him) came up with a far-out suggestion, "Why don't we walk a short distance down . . . the old swamp road."

"Are you nuts?" Robbie and I said in unison.

"I have a plan," suggested Gil.

"Well, let's hear it . . . but I'm not guaranteeing we'll do it," I said feeling a bit curious about the whole idea.

"Here's what we can do to make the adventure a little more safe but just as exciting. We will place a special stick along the road as far as we go on the first trip. Each time we explore the road, we will try to move the stick a little farther."

"That sounds like a super plan and I like the idea that it will be a little scarier than our other travels," blurted out Robbie in a very excited tone of voice.

I was still a little reluctant about the whole scheme because of the strange things that happened along that road in the past. Were these stories just people's imaginations running wild, or was there some truth to the tales of the "Swamp Creature"? After a minute or so I finally mumbled that I would go along with the idea as long as it was in daylight which didn't seem to be a problem since we all had to be home before dark even on Saturdays.

The reason I mention this is because we had decided to make our first trip down the road on this Saturday after breakfast. We could get our chores done later during the day after we returned.

That's *if* we returned, I thought. I have to admit, I was a little nervous about the whole thing. I could hardly sleep on Friday night. The day was almost here. Were we really going to test out this crazy idea? I guess so.

When morning arrived, I got dressed quickly, ate my breakfast and hurried off to our meeting place at the entrance to the old swamp road.

Everyone was there before me. I think we were all a little anxious to get this adventure underway before we changed our minds. Even though we weren't sure what the results would be, we were off down the road. Gil had the stick in his hand. He had carved our names into it with his penknife so we could easily identify it.

We were all happy to move along slowly. We were constantly looking into the swamp for any signs of trouble . . . especially if the stories were really true and there was a swamp creature that attacked people and dragged them off to its lair in the deep swamp.

We decided not to go too far the first day. Everything went well and we wanted to quit while we were ahead. We hadn't seen or heard anything unusual. Gil placed the stick at the side of the road and we retraced our steps back to the swamp road entrance.

Since it went so well the first day, we all decided that there was nothing to really be afraid off and that we would venture much farther down the road to the curve. The curve made us a bit nervous because once you made the turn, you could no longer see the road entrance.

On Monday night, before dinner, we made it all the way to the curve and left the stick. No problem. This adventure was not so scary after all.

On Tuesday night, we walked quickly to the stick and made the turn. It was a little spooky not being able to see the entrance, but we got over it. We went about fifty yards farther and placed the stick.

"By next Saturday we may be almost to the other side," Robbie exclaimed in a proud voice.

"Maybe," I said, "but let's not rush into things."

"Why are you always so skeptical, Stevie?" Gil responded. "We wanted an adventure and this one is turning out to be a lot of fun."

When we set out on Wednesday, we were all feeling very confident that we could move the stick quite a bit farther that night. When we arrived at our last finishing point, Gil picked up the stick and went, "Oooh, the one end of this stick is slimy."

I said in an unsure tone of voice, "Guys, I think the stick has been moved. We placed it back there by that broken—down palm tree."

Robbie murmured in a low voice, "I think we better call it a night and get out of here." Gil dropped the stick, and we raced back down the road.

"What are we going to do now?" I asked.

"Let's wait till Saturday before our next trip down the Old Swamp Road," Gil suggested. We all agreed.

When Saturday arrived, I wasn't sure that we would actually venture into the swamp again. What had moved our stick, and why was the stick slimy? Did someone see us go down the road and think it would be funny to try and scare us? These were all unanswered questions.

We all met at the road entrance as usual. We had decided to bring a backpack with medical supplies, a rope, a hunting knife, a compass, and food. We were worried about finding the stick. We were worried about a lot of things . . . but we walked on into the swamp.

We looked down the road, but the stick wasn't in sight. We cautiously made our way to the spot where we had found the slimy stick on Wednesday. We were right; the stick had been taken or moved. We searched the area, and then Robbie exclaimed, "Look, it's out there on that little island."

"Let's just get out of here," I demanded in a firm voice.

But the boys weren't moving. "I think we can wade through the swamp and get it," stated Gil, "it's not that deep. We can tie the rope to a tree and all hold onto it."

"I'm out of here," I barked.

"Don't be a chicken," they both said mockingly.

With that I started tying the rope to the tree. "Who's first?" I asked.

They couldn't act scared now, so Gil and Robbie both volunteered to go before me. Gil's plan seemed to be working well because we were about halfway to the island and there was no trouble so far. The swamp floor was a bit mushy and the water was dark and mucky, but we were making it across.

All of a sudden, Gil screamed. It was a large water moccasin was sticking its ugly head out of the water and baring its fangs. Gil had taken the hunting knife out of the backpack before we started across and it was a good thing he did. He waved the knife at the snake and we were surely in luck. The snake slithered off. In my mind, I knew it was still out there in the water and could return at any time. My nerves were on edge now. Was this all worth it? This was a bit more adventure than I bargained for.

If I thought the snake was scary, it was nothing compared to what we encountered on the little island. We hadn't noticed a thick bunch of bushes on the far side of the island. It seemed like there was something moving in the bushes. We were not going to wait around to find out what it was. We grabbed the stick and jumped back into the swampy water. The walking was difficult with the muck sticking to our shoes, but we hurried as fast as we could go. We were just about at the other side. Things were looking better. Just a few more yards to safely.

Then it happened . . . this ugly, slimy creature that looked half-plant and half-man appeared in front of us. It had its arms raised like it was coming our way. The muck was dripping off the creature, and we all realized that the legends were true. Why did we have to find out for ourselves? How could we escape?

I felt like I couldn't move. I was just about *scared stiff*. Our only chance was to dive into the three-foot-deep, murky swamp water and try to swim past the creature. With all that slime dripping off his face, maybe he couldn't see well and we could get by him. I held my breath and said to myself . . . here we go . . . I hope the snake isn't around. But the snake was the least of my worries—it was the swamp creature that scared me the most. He looked hungry and I might just be his dinner.

Once under the water, I knew this was a big mistake. I couldn't see a thing. It was pitch dark under here. But I had to give it a try or I was doomed. I swam underwater as best I could. I had to be near the land soon. Then I felt something grab me. Its hand was slimy. I fainted. When I awoke, I was lying on the Old Swamp Road with Gil and Robbie staring down at me. They said that they couldn't understand why I dove into that disgusting swamp water and tried to swim in it.

I said, "Didn't you see the swamp creature blocking our path?" They both looked at each other with confused looks on their faces.

"You must not be feeling well. You must have swallowed some of that swamp water and that made you see things," Gil said in a calm, understanding tone of voice.

They didn't believe me.

As I got to feeling better, I stood up and we started walking down the road toward home. "Let's try this again Monday night after school." Gil suggested. If they were going to explore the Old Swamp Road again it was going to be without me. I knew what I saw and I wasn't imagining things . . . or was I?

THE BABY SHARK

Our family was so happy. The in ground swimming pool that we all had been looking forward to had finally been installed. Even though there were still some muddy areas because of the digging and extra dirt, we were anxious to get on our suits and hit the water.

With the new pool, we suddenly became very popular with our neighbors. We were the only family in the neighborhood with an in-ground pool with a diving board, slide, and all. We knew we couldn't invite everyone, so we mainly entertained our closest friends in the neighborhood.

This idea did not set well with everyone, of course. There were three teenage boys who thought that they had as much right to the pool as anyone. We soon realized that whenever we were away, they would sneak over the fence and take a dip. We tried contacting their parents, but they were not any help. We tried contacting the police, but the police just couldn't catch them in the act. It became a very frustrating problem, because the boys did not just use the pool, but left empty soda cans and food trash around our patio area.

We decided it would be better if we forgot about this problem for a few days so we could enjoy our vacation at the seashore. We loved being at the shore as much as we enjoyed our new pool.

The day before we were to leave to go home from the shore an unusual event occurred right before our eyes. A fisherman had caught a baby shark. When he took it off the hook and placed it into a little pool of water . . . it began to swim around. Our whole family went down to get a closer look at it. Later in the day, the fisherman left the beach and said we could have the shark if we wanted it.

Why would we want a shark? Susie, my little sister, thought it would be fun to have a shark for a pet and begged to take it home. Mom and Dad said it would be okay for a little while until the shark got too big. We placed it into a large saltwater tank that we had set up in the family room. We had a great pet to watch.

Of course, while we were away our pool had been invaded by the teenage intruders. We could tell by the size of the footprints in the mud leading to and from the pool fence. What a pain they were. One time we almost caught them and Dad yelled after them to stay out of our yard and pool. The boys shouted back, "What are you going to do about it, old man?"

As the weeks went by, I noticed that the baby shark was getting bigger and bigger. What was my sister feeding it? Soon it was too large for the tank and Dad said we had to get rid of it. Sis asked Dad if she could keep it in the bathtub in her bathroom for a little while longer. I don't know how she did it, but she got Dad to say, "yes."

But this baby shark was growing bigger at an alarming rate. It wasn't a baby anymore. It was looking and acting downright dangerous. Dad and Mom decided it must go. The manager at the local aquarium said he would take the shark, but it could not come get it for two weeks. The shark was too big for the bathtub, so our only option was the pool. We stopped putting chemicals in the pool and were slowly adding salt. Finally it was suitable for the shark, which by this time was over four feet long.

With the shark taken care of, we were all going to spend the weekend at my grandparents' place. We liked visiting their house and playing in the fields and creek. Mom and Dad just liked the peace and quiet of the farm and we all liked Grandma's home cooking.

After a relaxing, fun-filled weekend, we drove back home on Sunday afternoon. We carried the suitcases into the house and hurried outside to check on the shark. To our horror, the pool was bright red . . . the color of blood . . . and there was just one visible sign of life . . . the moving shark fin sticking out of the bloody water. Dad noticed three sets of footprints leading from the fence to the pool, but only two returning to the fence. Dad said the boys must have seen the shark too late and panicked, but I thought that they must have been *scared stiff.*

DRAGON'S BLOOD

As we walked across the drawbridge that spanned the moat, I couldn't help but think that this old castle looked dangerous. But "danger" was not going to deter the Daredevil Detective Agency from solving its case. My name is Gordon but my friends call me "Gordo." Carlos is one of my friends, and he is bilingual. He is the one who gave me the nickname "Gordo" because I am slightly overweight and "gordo" means "fat" in Spanish. My mom gets my clothing in the "husky" department. In fact, all of our family would be considered slightly overweight.

My friends and I have formed this little detective club. We have all just finished fifth grade, and it is summer vacation. We like to solve mysteries or at least pretend we are solving them. Today, Alita, Louis, Carlos and I are about to enter an old abandoned castle. We are a diverse group, but this has never gotten in the way of our friendship and loyalty. For myself, I am usually not afraid of things or difficult situations or even abandoned castles for that matter, but this castle is known to be haunted.

I find out quickly that crossing the rickety wooden drawbridge might be the easy part of this adventure. It was what we encountered next that gives me the creeps. The hallway from the entrance to the courtyard is dark and dreary.

It is made of large stones like the rest of the castle. There are spider webs across the pathway that stick to your face when you walk into them. There is a little light coming from little windows that are high above our heads. This light casts eerie shadows on the walls. Louis asks in a hesitant voice, "Gordo, are you sure you know what we are getting into here?"

"No problem," I reply, "just follow me."

I lead our crew into the hallway and stride along confidently. What is there to be afraid of anyway? A few little spider webs can't hurt you. We enter the courtyard that makes up the center portion of the castle. We are surprised that it was nearly as large as a football field. These people must sure have been rich to afford this place. Twenty-foot high walls that were used as protection surround the courtyard. Some of the walls were crumbling down but some are still intact. Along the walls that are still complete are some of the remaining castle buildings. We are anxious to look inside these buildings. We really hope to find the castle dungeon. That place intrigues us the most. Maybe we could find out why this castle is claimed to be haunted or even better . . . what is actually haunting the castle. I really don't believe we would find such a thing, but detective agencies are supposed to solve mysteries and this is one we could look into anyway.

We see an opening into one of the buildings, and there are steps that lead down to somewhere. We decide to find out if this is the pathway to the dungeon. The steps are slippery and partly covered in moss. As we descend, it feels like we were entering a refrigerator. The passageway is getting darker as we get farther from the entrance. The steps begin to turn and I realized we are on a spiral staircase. We have to be heading for the dungeon. Nothing about this seems too safe, but we press on . . . downward . . . downward we creep in almost total darkness until . . .

"A-a-a-ah," I screamed as I feel myself falling into thin air. I hear my friends scream and I know they must be falling, too. What is going to be at the bottom of this fall? I am about to find out shortly. Thud, my body smashes into a solid stone floor of what appears to be the dungeon we were looking for. I ask, "Alita, are you okay?"

Alita moans, "I think my leg is broken."

"How about you, Louis?"

"I'm not sure, but I think I can walk. My legs seem to be just bruised," responds Louis.

"I'm okay, too," added Carlos. I'm glad Carlos is in good shape because he may have to carry Alita if she can't walk on her leg. Carlos is big and strong and nice enough to even carry a girl if he had to.

Louis speaks again and says in a worried tone of voice, "I'm scared. Where are we, and how will we get out of here?"

I am thinking the exact same thing and I am hoping that Louis could help us find the answer to his last question. Louis is very smart and his mind is always working overtime. His parents named him after the famous heavyweight fighter, Joe Louis. His parents are pretty clever too, because his name is Louis Joseph. But even when you are very smart, fear can play funny tricks even on the best minds. The object is not to panic. I try to stay as calm as possible even though I am worried that I might be spending the rest of my days in this dark, dank, death trap.

I decide to locate the others in the darkness by having them speak. I crawl on the floor to their voices. There is only a sliver of light coming from a window that is about fifty-feet above our heads. I don't want to fall into another crack. I don't think my body or mind could take it much longer. I was becoming *scared stiff.*

When we are all together I ask, "Alita, do you think you can crawl without hurting your leg too much?"

"I'll try," she responds hopefully.

We crawl along the edge of the walls looking for an escape route. The floor is slimy and awful to touch, but that is nothing compared to what I feel next. It feels like a human skull and when I hold it up to the little bit of light coming in the window I soon realize I am holding a real human skull. Before I can drop it, Alita screams, "It's more bones!" Then she holds up what looks to be an arm or leg bone with some of the flesh still on it. I feel sick and think I am going to throw up. I am hoping they aren't bones from other children who had been exploring this castle and had fallen into this horrible dungeon.

We are all freaked out by now and wish we had picked a different adventure for our detective agency. There seems to be no way out. We are just about to give up hope when we find it. It is a large bottle with a cork in the opening. We hold the bottle up to the light. What we read on the label on the bottle is even more shocking than finding the bottle itself. The label reads, "Dragon's Blood."

Carlos gasps and mutters, "Do you think we should open it?"

Alita suggests, "Maybe it's only water. I'm thirsty. Open it, and I'll taste it."

"Are you crazy?" I chide, "Didn't your parents ever tell you not to eat or drink anything if you weren't sure what it was?"

"Yes, but this is different. I'm thirsty and we're desperate," Alita replies.

Louis interrupted our conversation and says, "Let's make a pact that we will all taste the contents of the bottle no matter what happens." Foolishly, We all agree. Since it was her idea, Alita takes the first taste, then Carlos, then Louis, and then me.

As soon as the liquid touches my lips I know I have made a mistake. It is the most foul-tasting thing I've ever encountered. It is the consistency of blood but tasted like something not from this earth. As I look at the others I can see them turning . . . into . . . dragons. They are grotesque—looking with leathery skin and, they have small snakes growing out of their heads. They look like the ancient Greek monster, Medusa, but even more horrid.

They are scaring me, but I soon realize that by now I am looking exactly like them. The only things that don't change are our voices and our minds. We can still understand each other. The only problem with talking to each other is that sometimes small flames fly out of our mouths. We have to be careful not to burn each other.

After a few minutes, I notice that I have grown large leathery wings. This gives me an idea. "Let's fly up to the window and make our escape from this dungeon deathtrap," I suggest. We all agree to give it a try. I stand on my thin, spindly dragon legs, spread my wings, and start to flap them. To my great delight, I take off and soar into the air. I look down and Alita, Louis and Carlos are also in flight. We are on our way to freedom. We squeeze through the window opening by pulling in our wings. We are out in the fresh air over the courtyard of the castle. Our only problem now is . . . how do we get back to being our regular selves?

But before I can contemplate this issue for too long a bigger problem appears before me . . . it is a full-size, fire-breathing dragon and it looks angry! Its eyes are gleaming like two hot pieces of coal. I try to communicate with my friends and they all have the same idea . . . let's make a run for it! We all fly over the walls of the castle, but unfortunately the infuriated dragon is hot on our trail . . . and I do mean "hot' because he is bellowing flames of fire that shoot out about twenty feet. I can feel the intense heat on my leathery skin. The small snakes on my head are hissing like crazy. I don't know how we are going to escape this savage beast.

I decide our best chance might be on the ground because this monster of a dragon could fly much faster than us. The only thing that is saving us from being roasted dragon by now is that we kept changing directions quickly to avoid the fire breath. I scour the landscape below and suddenly a sight comes into view that could possibly be our salvation . . . it is a cave. I fly in that direction as fast as my wings would carry me. I like this ability to fly, but I don't like our life-threatening situation. This furious dragon is angry with us for some reason. Maybe he doesn't like anyone drinking his blood.

We fly easily through the opening of the cave and hope the giant dragon cannot fit through the opening. The fire-spitting beast lands outside the cave opening and roars, with fire sailing into the cave with each sound. The temperature inside the cave goes from cold to burning hot in a matter of minutes. I think I was going to melt.

I look at the entrance way and ponder trying to make an escape by attacking the dragon. Maybe we can take the beast if we have a three dragon to one advantage. But seeing the long, razor-sharp teeth and large curved claws, I know that isn't an option. We are destined to be fried dragon meat if something doesn't happen soon.

Before I can get that thought out of my brain it happens. The dragon's blood spell stars to wear off. We are all changing back to being ourselves. Is this a good or a bad thing at this point? Now I am just going to be fried "kid" meat instead of fried miniature dragon meat.

I am feeling hopeless when all of a sudden . . . poof, the dragon changes into a skeleton. This skeleton wastes no time and begins walking towards us. As it walks in our direction it is slowly growing a heart, lungs, and flesh. When it is finally in front of us we are all crouched up against the wall of the cave just about scared to death. This is all too much to comprehend.

It is then that I wake up with my two friends standing over me. Alita says, "I'm glad you are back with us."

Carlos adds, "You hit your head pretty hard on that low hanging stone in the hallway. You were out cold for about ten minutes."

"We were worried about you," Louis chimes in.

Boy, was I happy to be out of that dream. "Let's explore that hallway over there," I say as I get to my feet, "Maybe it leads to the dungeon."

THE HOUSE OF HORRORS

Today is our school field trip to the amusement park. I'm glad everyone sold all that candy so we can go. I know I sold a lot and ate a lot, too. Now we were finally here. The whole gang is excited about all the roller coasters and water rides. I am too, but I really want to stay away from "The House of Horrors" ride. Some people call these types of rides "Fun Houses" but I don't agree with that name. I want to have "fun," but without being scared half to death. I know it is just make believe and not real, but I would rather avoid that ride today if possible.

The day is starting off great with roller coaster after roller coaster ride, the flume rides, the flying swings, bumper cars, and plenty of food. We always seem like we are eating . . . popcorn, candy apples, ice cream, and hotdogs. Wow, I'm full.

Then it happens, Jimmy notices that the line for "The House of Horrors" was very short.

"Let's go," he says. Everyone is eager to make a dash for the ride but me.

I respond by saying, "Let's make that ride our last one just before we go home. They seem to like the idea, and in my mind I was hoping that they will forget about it until it is too late. I am safe so far.

We enjoy many of the other rides and it was getting dark . . . almost closing time. They have apparently forgotten about "The House of Horrors" and my secret fears are safe for at least another year.

That is until Kenny shouts, "What about 'The House of Horrors'? Let's hurry before we miss it." We get there and the young attendant tells us that this is the last ride and the park is closing. We all jump into the cars with two people in each. I'm still not sure if I'm ready for this but off we go into the darkness.

As we clank along, I am beginning to relax a little. How scary could it be? Then all of a sudden the first lighted exhibit appears out of nowhere. It is showing an operating room, and the crazy-looking doctor is using a chain saw to amputate people's limbs. I freak out. I have this funny feeling that these are real people and not mechanical robots.

We move to the next lit area and it is a cemetery with ghoulish-looking characters coming out of the graves. If they are trying to scare people, it is sure working. From some of the other cars, I can hear laughter and comments like, "This is so lame. Who could be afraid of this stuff?" I am feeling sick to my stomach by this time.

Just then the cars stop. It seems like the electricity has been cut off. I can hear screams coming from some of the other cars. I want to scream myself but nothing will come out of my mouth. Is this what real fear does to you?

I am hoping that they will either get the power back on real soon or come to take us off the ride. Neither of these things happens. The weird noises and screaming continue and no help is in sight. We decide we are on our own. But what is there to be afraid of? After all, it is just a ride. We crawl out of the car and carefully make our way along the tracks. As we head towards the entranceway, we pass the place where the graveyard setup is located. The graveyard is there, but the ghoulish zombies are gone. They must have been live people acting like monsters. Why panic now?

"Let's all make sure we stick together," I say in a panicked voice, "there is strength in numbers." I was just trying to reassure myself that we will be all right. We are on our way out and everything seems to be going fine . . . until the blood-curdling scream.

"Let's run for it!" Kenny shouts.

I am frozen like a zombie. My legs won't move. I am *scared stiff.* Kenny grabs me and I snap out of it. We sprint toward the door. But it is pitch dark. And we aren't really sure of the way. We crash into the walls. I feel my forehead and it is bleeding. Just then, something grabs me. It is a cold, boney hand. I scream. I'm a goner, I think to myself. I know I shouldn't have gone on this ride in the first place. I twist and turn to try to break loose, but it is no use . . . I pass out.

When I finally awake, my friends are all standing around me and looking down as I am lying there on a stretcher. I ask them what happened and they all just shake their heads and said, "You don't want to know." I think I do know . . . this is no ordinary Fun House and we sure didn't have much fun in it. I sure hope the police investigate this ride and the people who run this amusement park. All I know is that there will be no more fun houses for me. With that last thought, I am placed in the ambulance and I see the paramedics hovering over me. They have white masks covering their mouths and noses. I notice that they look a little strange to me . . . almost like the characters that were in the operating room on the "House of Horrors" ride. Could it possibly be? As I begin to scream, they put an oxygen mask over my mouth. I look up, and they have their masks off now. It is them . . . I'm their next victim.

THE MOST FRIGHTENING MASK

At our school we have a Halloween party each year. My name is Marcus and I love Halloween. This is my sixth year in school, and I have never won any of the prizes for best costumes or masks. The prize I always wanted to win was for the Most Frightening Mask. Unfortunately, in my class is Woodrow. His parents are very rich, and he always wins that prize. In fact, by now, he is pretty obnoxious about it. "Why do you other losers even try to compete with me? You know my dad will buy me anything I want."

He was right about that. Last year he bragged that his mask cost over a hundred dollars. I could never spend anywhere near that much for a mask and neither could any of my classmates. Most of the time I had to be contented with a mask made of papier-mâché that I made myself. I'm not complaining about making my own mask and costume. It was a lot of fun. It is a family project with my mom and dad helping my sister and me with our latest creations.

This year will be no different unless I can find a relatively cheap mask that is also very scary. I have saved some money from mowing lawns in the summer and hope that such a mask existed. I want one that is both realistic and scary. It can be an evil monster mask with a green face or an ugly witch one with a wart on the nose. I went to the usual stores at the mall and downtown, but nothing stood out. The ones I really like, I can't get close to affording. It looks like I will be wearing a good old papier-mâché mask again.

I usually don't read the advertisements in the newspaper but as I am leafing through today's edition, one ad especially catches my eye. The picture looks gruesome and the ad reads, "Most realistic masks in town. Reasonable prices. Stop in and try one on." The ad is for a novelty shop downtown. I have never heard of this shop before, but at Halloween there are lots of stores that are only open for a few weeks to sell Halloween costumes and other Halloween items.

I think that I might as well give it a try, so I get my money and head to town. It is only a few blocks to where the store is located. I know the address, but the store is not in the heart of town. I finally locate it way down near the end of the block. It is a rundown-looking store, and it appears a little creepy from the outside. But when I see the masks in the window, I know I had come to the right spot.

I enter the store and start to look around. The prices are more than just reasonable; they are downright cheap compared to the mall stores. As I am browsing, I'm startled by a short little man who has come out from the back of the store. He says, "May I help you find something?"

His voice is almost as strange as his looks. The voice sounds like it is coming from a machine or like someone is trying to change their voice on purpose. It also looks like he is wearing one of the masks, but I'm not quite sure. The man is very helpful. He shows me several special masks from the shelf behind the counter. He says these masks are the most realistic ones you could ever buy anywhere. He asks if I want to try one on. I choose the red mask that looks like a devil. It has horns that felt real and the mask is very pliable. It fits on my face like a glove.

Without much hesitation, I tell the old gentleman that I will take the mast. I know that this year I am going to win the contest for the Most Frightening Mask. It is a bit difficult getting the mask off, but I like the way if fit so snugly. It follows the exact contours of my face. This is a winner for sure. The man puts the mask in a bag, I pay him, and I am off for home.

I can't wait to show my parents and friends my new mask. I am really anxious for my class Halloween party this year. I especially want to see the look on Woodrow's face when I put on *my* scary devil's mask. But the party is still a week away, and I still have to make the rest of my costume.

My parents are shocked that I found such a realistic devil's mask for such a good price. I try the mask on for them, and they are even more impressed at my selection. "That thing looks like it form-fits to your real face," observes Mom.

"It does," is my reply. "It almost feels like my real skin." By this time, my two friends Dylan and Austin have arrived at my house. They both think my mask is terrific, and they want to get one at that shop, also. I figure it is okay because they are not in my class at school this year and their masks will not be competing with mine. I don't want to take any chances of losing the prize I want to win so much.

As I try to pull the mask off my face, I notice that it is even harder to get off than the first time I put it on. I try not to think about it and quickly start talking more about this unusual costume shop and the strange man that works there.

After hearing the story about the store, my parents are reluctant to allow me to go back there with only my friends. My dad says that he will drive us all to the store. Even my mom is curious about this place. We all jump in our van and we are off. As we drive down the street that the store is on, my dad asks, "Where is this place?"

I respond, "Down a bit farther near the end of the block." We drive on, but the store is not in sight. We do see the place where the store had been but it appears empty now. Why would they close the store before Halloween? It doesn't make any sense.

Dad pulls the car over and we all get out. We parade up to the window and peer inside. It is totally empty. I think I am cracking up . . . and so do my parents and friends. Dylan mutters, "Come on Marcus, tell us where you really got this mask."

"It was here. The store was right here! I exclaim. "I can't believe this."

"Let's get going," Dad suggests.

"I don't know if you should be wearing that mask anymore," adds Mom.

I do not think it is a good time to argue my case for wearing the mask, so I just keep quiet. But I *am* going to wear that mask in our classroom costume contest.

It is Friday and I have finally convinced Mom that my mask is safe and that I am sure to win the prize for Most Frightening Mask. I place my costume and mask in a paper bag and leave for school. The party will be in the afternoon. I make my friends and sister swear that they will not tell anyone about my mask . . . especially Woodrow.

All morning Woodrow is strutting around telling everyone about the great mask and costume he has for this year. "It cost over a hundred bucks," he boasts.

We are all sick and tired of hearing him brag and I can't wait till this afternoon so I can spring my mask on him. I am sure that would shut him up for a while at least.

Finally it is time to get our costumes on. No one is allowed to wear their mask outside of their own classroom for security reasons. The teacher leaves the room to get her costume on. All the teachers dress up, but they don't wear masks. I can think of a joke here, but I won't say it.

I keep my mask in my bag until the last possible second. When I have it pulled over my face, I hear several girls scream. This mask was about as real as you can get. I sit down in one of the other student's seats and the teacher comes back shortly after that. She looks around the room and starts to guess us. Some students are easy to guess and other kids have themselves completely covered. I am the last one guessed.

Now that everyone is guessed, we are going to have the judging for the different categories. We all put or masks back on. I don't have to because mine was already on. When I tried to get it off after I was guessed it seemed to be stuck to my face.

So far I haven't won any of the prizes, but I am waiting for that grand prize . . . the Most Frightening Mask category. It is the one that is always announced last. My time has finally come to put good old Woodrow in his place. The teacher holds up the trophy for Most Frightening Mask and in an eerie voice she says, "Marcus, that is one scary mask. It looks so real. You have won this year's prize for Most Frightening Mask."

Everyone cheers. I am as excited as I could be. Even Woodward comes over to me and says that he thinks I have the best mask he has ever seen. This is a great day.

Everyone is getting out of their costumes and getting ready for games and refreshments. I tug at my mask but it won't budge. It feels like it is glued to my face. Seeing that I am struggling, two of the parent helpers come over to help get my mask off. They yank and pull until it finally loosens up and comes off. They both scream.

Mrs. Miller, my teacher, turns and yells for me to get my mask off right now. I hate to tell her, but my mask is off. Was she just joking, and why did those women scream?

I find out quickly what the problem is. Mrs. Miller says to me, "Is this some kind of joke?" I don't know what she is talking about. "Why are you wearing red make-up under your mask?" she asks.

I am confused and just say, "What?"

"Go to the bathroom and wash that make-up off right away."

I am still not sure what she was talking about, but I do as she asks. I hurry into the boys' bathroom and look in the mirror. I scream myself. It is an ugly red-faced devil looking back at me. I quickly turn on the water and splash some onto my face. Nothing happens. I try a little soap and still the red coloring is there. I am starting to feel sick. Then I do something to ease my mind . . . I check my head to see if I am growing horns. To my relief, I can't feel anything. What am I going to tell my mom and dad?

I don't have too much time to think about it because my mom is already at the school. I hear my name on the loud speaker and I am supposed to report to the principal's office immediately. What a day. I go from the top of the world to the bottom.

I wait in the office while my mom goes to my classroom to get my things. She has my book bag and the bag with my costume. The mask is right on top. I swear is staring at me and smiling. My imagination must be getting the best of me.

I don't want to touch that mask ever again. I have to get rid of it. Maybe that will help get my face back to normal.

When my two friends come over they are shocked at what they see. "We heard about what happened in school," Austin says.

"But I didn't think it was this bad," adds Dylan.

"Thanks a lot," I respond dejectedly. "You guys have to help me get rid of this mask."

"We're not touching the thing," barks Austin.

"Don't worry, you guys won't have to touch it. I just want you to come with me."

"Okay, but where are we going?" asks Dylan.

"Back to the place where I bought it," I reply. "I am just going to leave it there in front of the store."

We walk to town and I try to cover my face with a ski hat and a scarf. So far so good. No one sees me and I don't have to answer any questions about my red face. We are in front of the store now and it still looks deserted. As I bend over to place the mask on the ground I notice a small light coming from inside. We push on the door and it opens.

"Are you going in there?" Dylan asks. "We're staying right here . . . on the outside."

"Okay, but I must go in," I said, "maybe the little man who owns the store has returned." I follow the light toward the backroom. There isn't anything in the front part of the store. It is a bit spooky, but who is going to bother me with my face looking like the devil himself.

When I reach the back room, I am in for my next big surprise. It's Woodward and his father sitting there.

"We have been waiting for you, Marcus. We knew you would be drawn back to this place," mutters Woodrow's father.

Was I dreaming again? What is this all about? I am totally confused by now. I look at Woodrow and in his hand is a mask. It looks just like the face of the little man who had sold me my mask. Things are starting to add up now. It was all an evil plan they cooked up to scare me half to death. Was that stupid Most Frightening Mask trophy that important, or was it that Woodrow was weirder than we thought? Woodrow's dad grabs me and makes me swallow some foul-tasting, green concoction. Immediately I feel like I am going to fall asleep.

The next thing I hear is a tramping noise and my two friends are looking down on me. They say, "Your face!"

"Oh, no. What now?" I gasp.

"You're back to normal!" they scream.

I sit up slowly and try to figure out what has just happened. Should I tell my friends about Woodrow and his dad? They will really think I was crazy then. I figure it is best to just keep things as they are. I am back to being my old self, I have won the trophy, and the mask is gone.

As we turn to leave, I notice that the mask of the old man is still lying there on the chair. Do these masks have some magical powers? They sure seem to. When the boys turn to leave, I pick up the mask and stuff it in my pocket. "Never know when this might come in handy," I think as I smile to myself.

The Neighborhood's Secret

It was a friendly little neighborhood where everyone knew each other. The children played along the streets and in the fields when the weather was nice. They had special events to celebrate the holidays. What a great place to live. But that all slowly began to change when the house at the end of the street was sold and an elderly man and his wife moved in. At first nothing seemed different. The people would see the woman working in her garden or walking to the store to get groceries. She would say "Hi!" to them as they passed her house.

But then things started to seem weird. The children no longer saw the woman out in the yard even though the weather was beautiful. She did not sit on the front porch and wave to them. They never saw her going for groceries . . . and they never saw the old man who lived there. The neighbors began to wonder what happened to the old woman. Where was she? And why didn't the old man ever leave the house? But, oh well, that was their problem. This still was a great place to live and raise children.

Things seemed to go along as they normally did until "that night!" . . . the night when little Johnny Wilson didn't come home. His parents looked frantically all over the neighborhood. The police joined the search, but to no avail. Johnny was never found.

The neighbors didn't want to be suspicious of the old man at the end of the street, but it was hard not to be. You see, his lawn and garden were now overgrown and the paint was peeling from his house. The nice fence around the yard was broken in places and the house started to look . . . haunted! The people living in the neighborhood would not allow their children to walk near the end of the street where the house was located . . . and they were never allowed to go out at night. Fear was starting to grip the community.

And then . . . things got worse. Another child disappeared. Panic and terror gripped the neighborhood. People were *scared stiff*. Something had to be done. Now was the time to find out what was really going on in the old man's house. The community members convinced the police that they needed a search warrant to examine the house. The police made up an excuse for the judge and the warrant was granted. Now it was time for the search.

As the police knocked on the door, they didn't know what to expect. The place looked almost deserted. It was dirty and smelled terrible. After what seemed like a long time, the old man finally answered the door. They showed him the search warrant, and he invited them in.

"Where is your wife?" they asked.

"Oh, she passed away last year," was his reply.

The police started to mumble to each other that no one ever mentioned that the wife had died or had seen anyone bring a body out of the house. Things were getting stranger by the minute . . . and scarier. Even having a policeman with a gun at my side, this place seemed unsafe. The police asked to see the house and the old man reluctantly showed them around. Nothing seemed really out of the ordinary except for the fact that the kitchen cabinets were empty and the refrigerator was not plugged in. What did this man eat? How did he stay alive if he never left the house? Those questions would soon be answered.

As the police were about to leave they noticed a door almost hidden in the far corner of the kitchen. It had a curtain pulled across in front of it. "What's in there?" the policeman inquired.

"Oh, nothing. It is just a closet", replied the man nervously.

Let's just take a peek in it before we leave. When they looked in . . . it was not a closet at all but some steps leading to the basement. Putting on their flashlights, they ventured slowly down the creaky steps. Now they knew why the place smelled so bad. The odor was overpowering. But what was that smell? We would soon find out. Slowly shining the flashlight around the dark, damp room the light fell upon a wooden table. As they got closer they could see the table was full of bloodstains and marks caused by a hatchet or axe. They also noticed another wooden door that looked like some sort of freezer. The police reluctantly opened the door not knowing or wanting to know what they were going to find.

"E-E-E-EK !! It's the children," screamed the police officer in horror," they're cut up. His wife is here too . . . or at least parts of her are here. He must eat them. That is why he doesn't shop for food. You're under arrest! Take him away."

The old man was placed in jail for murder and was to serve a life sentence. The neighborhood returned to being peaceful, calm, and carefree. The children played happily and even walked past the old man's deserted house.

Then something terrible happened. The people heard on the news that the old man had escaped from prison as was on the loose. In fact . . . he is HERE in the neighborhood right now . . . A-A-A-H-H !!!

THE CAVE GHOST

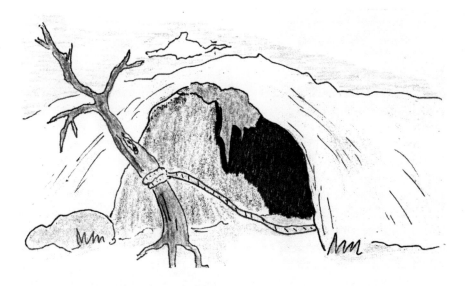

I always was fascinated with all the exciting things that the local Boy Scout troop planned for it summer outings. Some of the kids in school wore their Boy Scout uniforms and sashes with badges to school during National Boy Scout Week. I finally decided to ask Jack, one of the scouts, if there was any way I could go on one of their outings to see if I would like to join the Boy Scouts. He said that he would talk to his scoutmaster at their next meeting, which would be on Saturday.

On Monday at school Jack told me that they were having an outing next weekend where they would be exploring a real cave . . . not one of those commercial caves where you walk on paths and it is all lit up inside. This was a real cave where you would have to take a flashlight and at times crawl through the mud to get through. This sounded fantastic to me.

The next words out of Jack's mouth were the best. He said that the scoutmaster told him to invite me along to see how I would like scouting. I told Jack that I would ask my parents and then let him know tomorrow.

My parents liked the idea of my being involved in scouting. They believed Scouts taught young boys many good qualities . . . you know the scout oath and all . . . it goes something like I will always do my best to do my duty . . . and so on. They also liked the idea that scouting also provided many interesting opportunities for camping, hiking, and exercise . . . which my parents were always reminding me about. "Don't be a couch potato," they would say as I laid on the sofa and watched TV or played video games. The only thing they were a little leery about was this cave exploration.

My parents decided to call Jack's parents and check things out a bit further. Jack's dad assured them that I would be safe and that he was actually going along to the cave. He was a police officer and that made them feel a bit safer about the idea. He even offered to stop by and pick me up on Saturday to go to the cave.

With all those assurances, they consented to let me go spelunking or caving with the scouts. I couldn't wait till Saturday arrived. I got ready my sturdy hiking shoes, a flashlight, a sweatshirt (since caves are cold), and some pants that I could get muddy if necessary.

I'm up earlier than usual for a Saturday. In a little while Mom, Dad, and Billy are up and we have pancakes for breakfast. Billy is only six, but he is still begging Mom and Dad to let him go along, too. Of course their answer was, " For the tenth time, what part of 'no' don't you understand?"

"I think I hear the doorbell," I shouted as I jumped up from the table. Luckily I had eaten fast and was ready to go. I invited Jack and his father into the house to meet my parents. I heard my mom whisper to my dad about what a nice, polite boy Jack was and that the scouting must be working well.

"We have to get going if we want to be there on time," Mr. Jenkins said. And off we went toward the cave. The drive took about twenty-five minutes because the cave was on the outskirts of town.

At last we were there at Dragon's Cave. There were about twelve scouts and five adults in our group. The troop leader had already tied a heavy yellow rope to a dead looking tree near the entrance to the cave. He gave everyone very detailed instructions about what we were going to do and the safety rules. We had spare flashlight batteries and even some candles and matches. The scoutmaster had a small emergency kit in case anyone got a scrape or cut. Another thing that made me fell even safer was that one of the adults was going to sit at the entrance until we came out. He had a cell phone just in case we had to contact him.

"It looks like we are all set to enter the cave," the scoutmaster said at last. I was so excited I couldn't wait much longer without bursting.

First, the scoutmaster lowered himself down the rope about twenty feet to a level spot. Then several scouts went down and then another adult. Next it was Jack and then his dad. It was finally my turn. Going down the rope was a bit of a struggle since the stone slope was slippery, but I made it okay. Now we all had to get down on our stomachs and slither through a small opening. I figured if the adults could make it, it would be easy for me. We were getting pretty dirty from the mud. "Wow! This is really fun," I thought to myself.

I was holding my flashlight while I crawled, but all I can see is the roof of stone slightly above my head and Jack's father in front of me. At last we reach a large room in the cave. There are lots of stalactites and stalagmites to shine our lights on. I never thought I would see an uncommercialized cave firsthand. Now this is what I call real exploring.

Mr. Fredericks, the scoutmaster, asked everyone to be quiet because he wanted to tell us some information about caves. We learned about flowstone, columns, and many other interesting facts. Then he told us all to turn off our flashlights to see and feel how dark a cave really was. We were all supposed to be very quiet during "lights out" so we could hear if there were any bats moving about. James, one of the younger scouts, started to talk and the scoutmaster went "Shush" in a disturbed tone. Some of the others giggled, but I was starting to feel chills from the feeling of being alone. I knew I wasn't really alone, but it was pitch dark and you couldn't even see your hand in front of your face.

When we put our lights back on, the thing everyone wanted to know was how the cave came to be known as Dragon's Cave. He began by telling us that it came from an Indian legend about a brave who came into the cave to get away from some sort of monster. The brave never escaped, but he did leave some drawings on the walls of the cave.

"Can we see the drawings?" everyone asked at once.

"Sure," said Mr. Fredericks, "follow me." We moved toward the other side of the big room and he said for us to shine our flashlights across the lake that was in the center of this room.

And there it was . . . a drawing of what looked like a fire—breathing dragon. What a story! But the next thing that Mr. Fredericks mentioned about the legend was not quite as exciting. He said that the Indian's ghost still seemed to haunt the cave and that some spelunkers thought they heard and even saw the ghost. Some of the boys seemed to get a bit frightened. Darkness, a strange place, bats, eerie noises . . . that's enough to scare you silly.

But not me. I didn't believe in ghosts. But it sure makes a good story. Mr. Fredericks then gave all of the boys the option of returning the way we came in or taking a more difficult route out of the cave called the corkscrew. He said the other way was a little cramped and jagged at places. This sounded right up my alley. I just hoped Jack and his dad were up for the idea. When I asked them, they were a little skeptical at first, but eventually said, "Let's go for it!"

In fact, we were the only ones who went for it. Most of the others were somewhat afraid or a little tired by this point and just wanted to get outside and eat their picnic lunch. Mr. Fredericks said that he would wait for us at the place where this corkscrew tunnel reached the surface.

Mr. Jenkins said that I should lead the way with Jack next and him bringing up the rear. I don't know if I was just feeling brave or was being a little dumb when I crawled into the small opening with my flashlight leading the way. Mr. Fredericks said that it would be tight and he was right. Mr. Jenkins was struggling to get through some of the small spaces, but he made it. We were almost at the end because I could see a small patch of light from the outside up ahead of me.

As I got closer to the opening, I noticed that it was being blocked by something that wasn't made of rock. It looked like a pair of boots. I yelled at the person ahead of me, but there was no response. Was one of the parents just playing a trick to try to scare us? Now I could see that the boots were attached to a body, but I could not see the scoutmaster at the entrance. I yelled but no one answered. When I finally got close enough to touch the boots, I gave them a pull. To my horror, the boot came off and there was a bone for a leg. I screamed a blood-curdling scream. Mr. Jenkins and Jack asked me what had happened. I was so upset that I couldn't respond. Was this what it felt like to be *scared stiff*?

In a few seconds I recovered and tried to explain about the bony leg. Mr. Jenkins got out his cell phone and made a quick call. We were lucky that his call got through or we would have been stuck for a while. And the only reason the phone got any reception was because we were so close to the opening. Within minutes, the scoutmaster and the others were looking down at the decaying body that was blocking our exit. Most of the scouts did not want to watch as they pulled the body out of the opening, but I really didn't have much choice. "What a grotesque sight!" I thought to myself.

At last we were all out in the daylight. I still wasn't feeling that great, but it was much better than a few minutes ago. Oh, well, time to go down to the creek and wash up. My bag lunch was waiting. Mr. Fredericks had brought sodas and water for everyone. We all sat around on some logs and reminisced about our caving adventure. We had all gotten a bit more than we had bargained for, but we were not complaining. "Wait till I tell Mom and Dad," I thought.

We jumped into Mr. Jenkins's car for the ride home, but there was still one little detail that was bothering me and I had to find out the answer. As we were driving I asked Mr. Jenkins and Jack if they felt a very cold breeze whisk past them when the dead caver was pulled out of the entrance. They both said, "No, why?" I didn't want them to think I was still so scared that I was losing my mind, but I am sure that I saw a ghost fly by me and out the entrance. Maybe the ghost of Dragon's Cave is free at last.

DEAD MAN'S CURVE

"Come on! What are you . . . a chicken?" yelled Rocko in a taunting voice. Rocko liked to get his own way, and since he was much bigger and stronger than the rest of us, he usually did. He had a tendency to brag about all the things he could do better than us and was always challenging us to do things that were a little dangerous or probably against our parents' wishes. This challenge was about sledding.

Our group of neighbor boys liked to play football, baseball, ice hockey . . . just about anything. We all got along very well, except for Rocko. He bothered each of us on one occasion or another. You never knew when it would be your turn next. The few times that someone stood up to him, they were usually pinned to the ground and humiliated until they said "Uncle." For this reason we just gave in without too much fuss, but we all resented the situation.

Rocko's challenge was of the usual kind . . . racing to the bottom of the hill on our sleds. It was a long hill that began on the playground and ended up by going through an undeveloped part of the church cemetery. At the very bottom was a creek that was frozen solid by this time of year. It was long and spine-tingling ride and we all loved it. But racing against Rocko would take away some of the fun. It was just another time for him to show off at our expenses.

Rocko announced to everyone that he would give us all a head start and still beat us easily. He did have a sleek-looking sled and his extra weight made him slide along a lot faster than the rest of us smaller guys. All that didn't matter because we didn't want to hear the word "chicken" for the rest of the day.

As usual, Rocko beat us all to the bottom of the hill with relative ease and was standing there gloating when we finally arrived. "When will you guys ever beat me at anything?" Rocko announced, "I'm getting tired of beating this tired-looking group without even trying." We all just turned around without a word and started the long haul of pulling our sleds back up the hill.

I was cold and had enough sledding for one day. And besides, tomorrow was Christmas. I couldn't wait because I was expecting a special present . . . a new Flexible Flyer sled. It was the best one made and no one in the neighborhood had one like it.

The next morning, I looked at my presents and didn't see anything that was shaped like a sled. 1 was a little disappointed. I opened a few boxes of clothes and books, but they weren't what I really wanted. Then I opened a box and in it was a note. The note said that I should go to the garage for a big surprise. And there it was leaning against the wall . . . a long, powerful looking Flexible Flyer sled. I couldn't wait to show it to my friends.

After breakfast, I put on my snow outfit and was off to the playground hill. I knew everyone would be there to tell each other about their new presents. The guys were all gathered around talking when I arrived. Everyone was there except Rocko. I was glad he wasn't there yet. I pulled my new sled along behind me. When I joined the group a couple of the guys just whistled. "What a great looking sled!" exclaimed Reggie.

"Wow! That looks really fast," chimed in Joey.

"It doesn't look so fast to me," came a voice we knew was Rocko's. "If you think it's so fast, Big Shot, let's you and me race to Dead Man's Curve."

All of my friends gasped. "Don't do it," said Joey, "it's too dangerous."

Of course, the next words out of Rocko's mouth were, "Buck, buck . . . chicken. Are you always going to be a CHICKEN?"

I had to meet the challenge this time. I hadn't tried out my new sled yet, but I was counting on it. It could mean life or death, though. You see, the Dead Man's Curve was a sledding spot that most younger people avoided. It was a sharp curve that had a wall of stone on one side and nothing but a steep drop on the other. It had enough room for two sleds but just barely. The key was to get to the curve first and take the track next to the wall. Because one little bump and the sledder on the inside would be off the edge and fall about forty feet onto a pile of broken tombstones and other jagged rocks. This is why it got the name Dead Man's Curve. We heard of many kids who had gotten badly hurt sledding the curve, and even one legend tells of a boy who died on the way to the hospital.

I must have been crazy, but I was lining up with Rocko for the race. Of course, this time there would be no head start. "Come on, baby, show me your stuff," I whispered to myself as I flopped onto my sled at the start of the race. All of the boys took off right away to take the shortcut to get to Dead Man's Curve before us.

The sled was working just fine. I could see that Rocko had a slight lead, but I was right on his heels. The flexibility of my sled was giving me a slight advantage on the turns and this was making up for Rock's weight and strength advantages. I peered up ahead and saw it. We were approaching Dead Man's Curve. It looked like I might beat Rocko there because I had just passed him on the last turn. As I went by, I heard him shout, "You don't have the guts to take on the curve! Give up now before you get hurt."

You know, I had this funny feeling in the pit of my stomach. I wasn't sure if it was fear or the taste of victory. Did I detect a bit of worry in Rocko's voice back there? Was he worried about his reputation and was he trying to scare me out of the victory I had earned?

No matter what that feeling was telling me . . . I entered the curve. But I didn't take the high side next to the rocks, but the low side next to the edge. I knew that the low side route was shorter and it gave me a better chance to win. The curve was sharp and steep. I felt like I was flying. In a split second I was flying . . . flying right off the edge of the cliff. Rocko had caught up to me. I felt his hand push on the back part of my sled and I knew I was a goner. I could actually hear him laugh and yell, "Sucker!" as he continued down the curve.

All of my friends cried out in fear. "Oh, no, what did you do, Rocko?" They had all seen what he had pulled and were *scared stiff*. Was winning that important to him that he would risk someone's life?

But miracles do occur . . . and this was sure a good time for one. As I sailed through the air, my sled seemed to be floating on wings. The sled turned a little and the next thing I knew I landed with a thud . . . right on the trail at the bottom of the hill. I slid forward a few yards and crossed the finish line way ahead of Rocko. Even with his cowardly maneuver, he had lost. I had won.

When Rocko did arrive, none of the boys would talk to him. He had lost more than the race . . . he had lost us all.

OUR WEIRD SCIENCE TEACHER

Moving from elementary school to the middle school is a scary proposition for many fifth grade students. I felt like I was different. I was really looking forward to changing classes, meeting new classmates, and having a real science lab to do exciting experiments.

The time had finally come; it was the first day of school at last. The summer vacation has a lot of nice qualities and I enjoyed the time to do anything I wanted, but after a while it does start getting boring. I love to learn new things and school is just the place to do that.

I have been assigned to a homeroom teacher named Mrs. Barrigan. She is at least sixty, but very nice and friendly. We all get our schedules, and I find out that I have science the last period of the day. Science is my favorite subject even though I'm a girl. Some people say that science is for boys, but I don't buy that . . . girls can do anything!

The day seems to go by quickly, and at last it is science class. I can't wait to meet my teacher. All of my other teachers have ranged between excellent and all right.

Boy, did we all get a shock when the science teacher walked out of his little office at the back of the room. His hair looked like he copied his style from

Albert Einstein. But that wasn't the end of it. He wore a bow tie with his white lab coat and tied his black, high-top, Converse sneakers with electrical wire he must have found in the lab kits. He was a sight to be seen.

This was either going to be an interesting year in science or a total disaster. Soon we would find out. Mr. Webb introduced himself and told us that he used to work in a real science lab and did experiments with all kinds of animals. That sounded pretty good so far. In fact, as he spoke I realized he was very knowledgeable about biological science and was a bit funny to boot. This could prove to be an interesting year in science after all.

One student asked him if we were going to do any experiments, and he said, "Lots of them." Wow! We all couldn't wait to get started.

Soon the bell rang and we were off to homeroom for the daily announcements and then to our lockers. My first day was a great one and I was looking forward to the rest of the year . . . especially Mr. Webb's science class.

Every week we did at least one science experiment and they were fun. I was really learning a lot about science and enjoying it in the process. Mr. Webb did have some unusual quirks that showed up from time to time but for the most part he was pretty normal. On one occasion he did ask for a volunteer to help him with one of his many demonstrations and the student did get sick enough to have to go to the nurse's office. We didn't think anything of it and just thought maybe the kid was sick already.

Near the end of the school year, Mr. Webb announced that we were going to do a major project to find out the effects of certain foods on humans. He promised us that we would not be eating anything harmful. He had brought in many technical instruments to measure blood pressure, heart rate, allergic reactions, and muscular dexterity, and more. He told us that this is what real science in the outside world was like. We were all eager to participate. We all had to bring in signed permission forms and everyone did.

The first few experiments were a lot of fun. We ran on a treadmill with wires attached to our arms, and Mr. Webb recorded the readings shown on the dials. We all had our own chart with our scores recorded. On the last day of school we were going to have our final project test. We all were given unfamiliar things to eat. I was thinking what our health teacher had told us, " Don't eat anything if you are not positive what it is." Should I trust Mr. Webb and eat these things?

I wasn't sure what to do, but when everyone else was trying the wild mushrooms, I decided to join in. These sure tasted great.

After about ten minutes, everything started to look a little blurry. I could see some of my classmates lying on the floor. They looked like they were asleep. I was fading fast. I saw Mr. Webb put some green florescent liquid in some of the students' mouths. I noticed that Mr. Webb had turned an unusual color of green and his skin looked like it had bumps all over it. Was I imagining things? What was this potion doing to me? I was almost completely gone now. But before I was totally out, I heard Mr. Webb say, "Great, now I have about twenty more slaves to take back to planet Xeron with me. Since I got this job, it has been easy to get these earthlings to take the potion. Now all I have to do is call for a teletransporter."

I wasn't sure if Mr. Webb had given me the potion or not. Did he take everyone, or only those with the best test results?

In a few minutes, I was awake again and sitting up. Mr. Webb was helping students to their feet. He said, "That must have been a bad batch of mushrooms. I hope everyone is okay."

Most students nodded and took their seats. A few were still a bit groggy and needed to be helped. I was running everything through my mind. Did I imagine that I heard Mr. Webb talking to himself while we were supposed to be knocked out? Oh, well, I felt fine now and everyone else seemed to be fine, too.

Well, it was back to homeroom and the end of another year has come at last. Mr. Webb was quite strange, but his class sure was interesting.

As I walked out of school, I did notice that some of my classmates seemed to be acting almost like robots. That's unusual for the last day of school. I thought that they would all be hurrying toward the door. Something was strange here. To relieve my mind, I thought that I would just drop by and say good-bye to Mr. Webb one more time. Maybe I was still letting my imagination get the best of me. I looked in Mr. Webb's room, but after what I saw I decided not to enter. Mr. Webb looked like he had a special chamber set up and was placing students, actually some of my classmates, in it one-by-one.

I was just about to leave when Mr. Webb turned around and saw me. "Come on in, my prize science student," beckoned Mr. Webb. For a moment I just stood there *scared stiff* at what I saw. But when he started moving toward me, I bolted for the nearest exit out of the building. I heard Mr. Webb mumbling after me, "I'll get her next year."

I'm thinking about changing schools in the fall . . . wouldn't you?

The Curse of
the Pirate's Treasure

Living near the seashore has its advantages and disadvantages. My parents are always worried about hurricanes ruining the house. That may be the only disadvantage in my book. The Florida beaches are wonderful almost every day of the year. We live only two blocks from the ocean and the beaches have become the playground for my buddies and me.

We all love to swim, ride our surf boards, and fish. Many days we just walk up and down the beach looking for things. You cannot image the variety of useful items people either forget or just plain throw away. We have been collecting these things for a year, and the ones that are good enough or repairable we try to sell on sunny days. We have been quite successful, and our little beach stand has provided us with some necessary spending cash.

Our stand is really just a card table and a couple of beach chairs, but it is at a great location where many people enter or leave the beach. We only have it open a few hours of the day when we are not in school during the summer and most Saturdays throughout the rest of the year.

My dad likes the idea that we are learning about the world of business at a young age. He always says that hard work pays off. My dad actually has a lot of these sayings that he uses from time to time. But, I don't mind because they usually prove to be true. He has lots of life experiences from traveling all over the world with his job. That can have a downside to it too, because he is away sometimes for a week of two at time. I miss him a lot when he is away because we do lots of things together when he's here with me.

I have a little sister, Kathi, that misses him when he is away. She loves it when he tells her stories about his adventures. I like to listen to these stories too, even though I know that my dad exaggerates them a little to make them more exciting and interesting.

Mom is a great cook and we all love the delicious meals she prepares for us especially when Dad is at home. Mom is usually around most of the time except for the few hours a week she works in a law office. She says it gets her out of the house and provides our family with a little extra vacation money.

I think about what it would be like to be really rich like Bill Gates, but I know that probably will never happen to me. But anyone can dream and as my dad says, "If you are going to dream, dream big. Hard work can make dreams become reality." I guess my dad feels the time the boys and I spend on our little business venture is time well spent, and we are on our way to becoming successful young men in the future.

Today started out just like every other day, but it sure didn't end that way. Ryan and Jeff were at my door at eight o'clock sharp and we were off to scour the sand for any items left behind after the beaches closed last night. We found a few plastic buckets and some shovels, but nothing too exciting. We all took a quick dip in the ocean, dried off, and sat on the beach thinking of what we wanted to do next.

We decided to spend the rest of our time until ten o'clock exploring around the state park. It was located at the place where the beach curved inward toward the bay. You were not allowed to bathe or picnic there, but you were allowed to walk on the beach and also explore the scrub pine forest area adjacent to it. We had done this plenty of times and it was fun because we always made up a little adventure story to make it seem more exciting.

Today our story theme was going to be about pirates. Since it had rained pretty hard last night, we pretended that a pirate ship had been shipwrecked on the beach and that the pirates were roaming around looking for a place to bury their treasure chest full of gold coins. Sometimes we would play hide and seek with one person being the bad guy and the other two of us hiding. Today we pretended that one person was going to hide a treasure chest (actually the bucket we had found) and the other two would try to find it with the pirate giving us clues of hot or cold. If we got closer he would say hot and if we got farther away he would say cold. The game was just great.

When it was my turn to hide the treasure I decided to walk along the shoreline where some of the beach had been washed away. When I saw it I couldn't believe my eyes. There it was sticking partially out of the sand . . . a real looking pirate's treasure chest. Was I seeing things? I went over and touched it and, it was real.

I immediately yelled to the boys to come over here quick. I told them I had found a real treasure chest. "Yeah, right," yelled back Jeff, "we're not going to fall for that old trick."

"No, really, it's here in the sandbank!" I screamed back, "get over here right away before the tide comes in."

When they arrived they both said, "You weren't joking with us this time. It is some kind of wooden chest."

"Let's use our shovels and dig it all the way out," panted Ryan. He was out of breath from running over. He should get himself in a little better shape. Jeff and I did most of the digging, and we managed to get the chest loose before the tide moved in too far. It was heavy, though, and we couldn't lift it.

"We will have to open it right here," I said.

"No way!" Ryan responded. 'It might have a curse on it. I read about pirates who put curses on their treasure boxes and anyone who opened it would suffer the consequences."

"I don't believe in curses," stated Jeff emphatically. 'Let's pry it open right now. I can't wait to see what is inside."

"It is pretty heavy," I said. "I hope it isn't just filled with sand."

"Open it then," chimed in Ryan. "Get it over with."

We struggled to get the lid open, but when we did we were pleasantly surprised. In fact we were in a state of shock. The chest was filled with gold coins. We picked them up and examined them. They felt good sliding through our fingers. Could this treasure put me in the category of Bill Gates? Would we be able to claim this treasure?

While two of us stayed there to guard our treasure, Jeff ran home to tell all of our parents what we had found. At first they didn't believe him, but he was acting so excited they all made the trek down to the beach. They could see us ahead and we waved a few coins at them. This got them to speed up quite a bit.

When the parents finally reached the treasure chest is when Ryan noticed the note. He picked it up, unfolded it, and began reading:

Beware! There is a curse on this gold. It belongs to me and me alone. If you touch it, you will feel my curse.

Blackbeard the Pirate

Ryan was scared stiff. He couldn't move. Finally he said, "I knew it. I knew that pirates put curses on their treasures. What is going to happen to us?"

"Nothing," I blurted out. "We are all rich."

The adults carried the treasure back to our house. My dad said that we had to call the police and try to find out the story behind this treasure chest full of gold coins. We all moaned because we were sure that we weren't going to see a penny of the money.

When the police arrived we showed them the treasure chest and the pirate's note. Just about that time; Jeff, Ryan and I started to itch all over. The itching was rapidly getting worse.

"I told you so," yelled Ryan, "the curse is starting."

The police officer told my parents that he would have to check into things, but if this was really a pirate's buried treasure . . . it was all ours. Even though we were itching like crazy, we all screamed "Wow!" at once. I could put up with a little itching for this kind of money.

The police took several coins along to get them authenticated by a coin specialist. They were careful to use plastic gloves . . . just in case the curse was real.

Meanwhile our moms put cream on our bodies to lessen the itching. While we were waiting for the phone call from the police, Dad put on the local news and weather. The first thing we heard was that there was a beach warning for today that no one was supposed to go in the water because there were too many jellyfish.

Boom, it hit me like a rock. I yelled, "That's it! That is why we are itching so much. It is not because of the curse. It is because of the jellyfish."

We all felt relieved, but Ryan felt the most relieved. Now all we had to worry about is if the treasure would really be ours. Even if it isn't, it was the best adventure we ever had.

A ROBBERY IN
THE MUMMY ROOM

Everyone in our class loved field trips. Even though we knew that we were taking them for the educational value, most of us had it in the back of our minds that it was mainly a day off from school. There would be no books, no reading, no writing . . . just plain fun was on the agenda for today.

Cory, Benji, and I were determined to have the most fun. Our teacher had very strict rules for field trips, but we were not going to let them deter our adventures. Everyone had to have a partner and each group of six students was assigned to an adult chaperone. No group or individual was to move to a new room in the museum unless everyone in our class was moving. There was to be no wandering around on our own, and we were definitely told to keep out of trouble.

Even with all these rules, this was going to be an exciting trip for our class. Mrs. Detmer, our teacher, was teaching us about early Egyptian civilization, and she told us that this museum had a real mummy that we would be seeing. The Mummy Room was the museum's main attraction, and everyone could not wait to see it. Well, almost everyone that is. Some of the students did not cherish the idea of coming face-to-face with a person who has been dead for several thousand years. From what we have heard, it is a grotesque sight. The face is shrunken and turning a dark shade of brown from age. It seems to stare at you and say, "Why did you do this to me?" This didn't bother me though. I was anxious to look upon the sickening face of a real mummy.

Besides the mummy, the Mummy Room contains many other Egyptian artifacts. A few of the items had been borrowed from the King Tut collection that resides in the Cairo Museum in Egypt. These items were extremely valuable and there were guards at the entrance and exit of the room. They did not want to take any chances on these items being stolen.

As we moved from room to room Cory, Benji, and I were enjoying the sights but were all feeling that we would like to sneak ahead of the class to the Mummy Room. We came up with a plan to all ask to go to the bathroom at the same time. Then we would sneak off for a quick peek at the mummy. It sounded like a foolproof plan to all of us.

So far so good, I thought. We all got permission to use the lavatory which was close by. We were told that the class would meet us in the next room. Perfect. We had some time to play with. We could go to the bathroom, see the mummy, and be back without anyone missing us.

Well, as many great plans go, we ran into a snag . . . and what a snag it was. We had all gone into one stall to finalize our plan, when the museum alarm went off. The very next second, three older boys ran into the bathroom. We did not make a sound. We actually all tried to get our feet off the floor in case they looked under the stalls to see if anyone else was in the bathroom. Even though our stall door was closed, these boys didn't check it because they knew that younger students loved to lock the stall doors and then crawl out underneath it.

We were silent as a bunch of mice. We strained our ears to try to hear what they were saying. The three of them were in the last stall closest to the wall. One of them said, "I got the gold jewelry from the Tut exhibit. Let's put it in this plastic bag and tie it inside the toilet tank. We will come back tomorrow and pick it up. Billy, you did a great job distracting the guard by pretending you were sick. It gave us time to break the glass and grab the jewels before he got back to his post."

One of the other boys whispered, "Let's do it quickly and get back out to our class. No one will suspect us."

A few seconds later, they were gone. Rather than going over to get the jewelry ourselves, we decided to run and tell our teacher. If we were carrying the bag of stolen jewelry, they would have thought we had taken it.

We finally located our class just as the teacher was taking a head count. Panting and excited, we tried to all talk at once. "Slow down, boys," demanded Mrs. Detmer, "only one speak at a time."

"We know who took the jewels and where they are."

"What?" exclaimed Mrs. Detmer in disbelief.

"Really, we do know. We were in the bathroom and overheard these three older boys planning to hide the King Tut jewels that they had taken. It seemed like they were planning this heist before they arrived at the museum. They had a plastic bag and string to tie the jewels inside the back of the toilet," I hurriedly explained.

Mrs. Detmer and the others seemed in shock. "We have to tell the security guards!" I screamed.

"Yes, good idea," said Mrs. Detmer who had seemed to recover from the initial shock.

She and one of the parents took the three of us to find a guard. This was easy because they were all over the place by now. The alarm was still sounding and the museum was on lockdown. This meant that everyone would have to be searched before leaving the building. The older boys plan seemed more brilliant all the time. They did not care if they were searched today, because they were coming back tomorrow to pick up their goods when they wouldn't be searched.

It was brilliant, but not brilliant enough. They had never figured on anyone else being in the bathroom. They were just not careful enough. We were going to get them. I could recognize their voices anywhere.

Mrs. Detmer told the security guards what we had told her and they followed us to the bathroom. "It's hidden in the back of the tank in the last stall," I said confidently. The boys and I would be heroes. Maybe there might even be a reward. Maybe we would get our pictures in the newspaper.

Just when everything seemed to be going so well, I heard the security guards say, "There's nothing here."

"What?" I shouted in a panicked voice, "there has to be."

"Look for yourself," said the guard sounding a little annoyed. I did, and he was right, there was nothing there. Mrs. Detmer gave us the meanest look and we were out of there. She thought we were making the whole thing up.

"Young boys have such wild imaginations," I heard her say to one of the parents.

We were all embarrassed and humiliated. We all got searched on our way out and got on the bus. It was a pretty silent ride on the way home thanks to us. Our exciting adventure to the museum sure did not turn out as I had expected. But as that famous baseball player, Yogi Berra, once said, "It's ain't over 'til it's over." And in my mind this was not over by a long shot.

When we got off the bus, I gathered Cory and Benji close to me. "Meet me at the museum at opening time tomorrow," is all I said. They knew what I was planning to do.

I could hardly sleep especially after I told my parents what had happened. They really tried to believe me, but I could tell there were doubts in their minds. Oh, well, tomorrow I would prove to them and everyone else that we were right. But where were the jewels? They had to be in that bathroom somewhere.

The next morning the newspaper headline was "King Tut jewels stolen from the Mummy room." It also stated that there were no suspects and no clues. I was thankful it did not mention anything about me.

The boys and I were the only chance the museum had of recovering the jewels and catching the thieves. We all met outside just before it opened and entered the museum before anyone else. We were going to hide in the bathroom stall until the other boys arrived to pick up the jewels.

After an hour or so we were definitely getting a little tired of being cooped up in this small stall with nothing to do. We were afraid to talk in case the boys came in. Cory wanted to give up the idea, but I convinced them both to wait for another half hour and then we would head home.

The time was still passing slowly when we heard our first sign of life. Someone had entered the bathroom, but it was a false alarm. It wasn't the thieves. Just as we were about to open the door to leave, it happened. In sped three boys speaking in whispers. One said, "Billy, get out your screwdriver and get busy. We will guard the door and signal you if someone is coming."

We were afraid to look out to see where they had hidden the jewels, but soon we realized that Billy was in the last stall again and standing on the back of the toilet tank. He reached up and removed the screws from the air conditioning vent by the ceiling and pulled out the plastic bag.

"I got it," he said in a low voice.

"Good, let's get out of here," the oldest boy replied.

Now what were we going to do? We knew who the thieves were, but how were we going to stop them while they still had the stolen goods?

Well, some of your best or worst plans come to you in a split second and you just do them on impulse. This was one of those times. I stuck out my foot from under the stall and unsuspecting Billy tripped right over it. We opened the door and grabbed the bag of jewels he had dropped.

But that is about as far as we got. The other two boys were now blocking the doorway and moving toward us. By now Billy was on his feet and had his penknife in his hand with the blade in full view. We slowly backed up as far as we could until our backs were pinned against the wall. As the boys and the knife moved closer, I lost all my powers to think. I was *scared stiff* and so were my two friends.

The three boys were not talking and we were too scared to scream. What were they going to do to us? We had seen their faces and heard two of their names. They could easily be tracked down by looking at the class lists from yesterday's museum visits. I was losing all hope of survival. Me and my great detective ideas have gotten us into a big jam this time.

Bang!!! The bathroom door flew open and the security guards charged in with their guns drawn. I don't know at this point if I was more scared now or more relieved to see them. The three boys turned around and realized they had no way out. The security guards grabbed them, took the bag of jewels, and ushered them out in handcuffs.

The head security guard remained behind and asked us, "Are you boys all right?"

We all murmured, "Yeah, I guess so."

Then I asked him how he knew to come into the bathroom just at the right time.

He told us that they had been watching us since we entered this morning. They were also watching the older boys who were looking very suspicious as they wandered around the museum for the second day in a row. "When they entered the same bathroom as you boys did, we got ready to rush in if we heard any commotion", the guard said. "And when we heard the boy hit the floor, we decided we better enter real soon."

"You were just in time," I said with a sigh of relief.

The guard then led us out to his office and asked us to tell him what happened. When we were finished he said with a big smile on his face, "Well, I should have listened to you young detectives more closely yesterday and we may have avoided all this trouble for you today. I know there is a hefty reward for the return of these jewels and the newspaper reporter and photographer are on their way to get some pictures and your story. You boys are real heroes."

This time I will be happy to have my picture in the paper and I sure hope they spell my name right. I want all the kids at school to see that I wasn't making it all up after all.

The Mothman Escapes

It's that special time of year for all fifth grade students . . . it's time to go to camp. As part of our study of ecology and animal habitats, we have a three-day camping experience. It is usually one of the highlights of fifth grade. I know it will be for me. I love the outdoors.

I'm Alita, your typical tomboy. I have two older brothers and I always wanted to do what they were doing. I played football, baseball . . . just about everything with them and their friends when they needed another person to make the teams even.

Now we were getting ready to go to camp. We had several lessons in class to prepare us for the adventure. We learned about first aid, poisonous plants and snakes, and other valuable information that would give us some background information before we actually got to the camp. I was ready.

The couple of days before we were to get on the bus to the local YWCA camp, we were given a list of what to bring and what not to bring. We were **not** allowed to bring electronic games, cell phones, food, or penknives. I had just about all the things I was allowed to bring already packed. I couldn't wait.

Wednesday finally arrived and we were on our way to camp. It was only about a thirty-minute ride, but when you got to the camp you felt like you were in the middle of the wilderness. The lucky boys got to sleep in cabins, but the girls were all packed into the lodge. We had plenty of room, but it did not feel quite as adventurous as being in a cabin.

After we got unpacked we had a guided tour of the camp facilities. The teacher in charge, Mr. Fry, told us that it was almost impossible to get lost. He said all you had to do is just keep walking downhill until you reached the road and then walk along the road to the camp. He also said that we were never to venture very far out into the woods alone. Even during quiet hour we were to be relatively close to the lodge.

The lake was another area that had a lot of rules. Of course, our safety was always the main concern. We would have opportunities for canoeing, fishing, and water study that would revolve around the lake. We had a lifeguard on duty at all times and high school counselors were assigned to each group of six students. They were with us most of the time.

The camp activities were well planned and kept us busy from morning 'til night. By the time we got in bed the first night, we were all pretty tired. We had hiked, had an art lesson in which we made colorful camp tee shirts, had a volleyball game, canoed, fished, hiked some more, did an obstacle course, and finished up with a night hike and treasure hunt using flashlights. It was a full and enjoyable day. I couldn't wait till tomorrow. After a little chatter time, the counselor turned the lights out and asked us to be quiet. I fell asleep quickly as did most of the others.

The next day was as much fun as the first and maybe even a little more. One of my favorite activities on this day was the Marine Hike. While on the trail, Mr. Fry asked our group if we wanted to take the Kindergarten Trail or the Marine Hike. Of course we all shouted, The Marine Hike. We said this even before we knew what it was going to be like. Mr. Fry had us crawling under and over logs, climbing steep hills and then sliding back down, walking on a log over a small stream, building a dam, and many other challenging but exciting things. It was right up my alley. I was the first girl to volunteer to do most of the tests. I would even try it before the boys if I were asked.

For the evening meal we had a cookout with hot dogs, baked beans, potato chips and my favorite . . . s'mores. S'mores are made up of melted marshmallows placed on a piece of chocolate and squeezed between two graham crackers. They were delicious.

The next event was just about everyone's least favorite. It was shower time. After our showers we all met in the great hall of the lodge. It was called the Elk Room for the obvious reason that it had a large elk head hanging over the fireplace. At this time we watched two movies about animals, plants, and conservation. After the movies we had some snacks and then it was time for ghost stories. We turned out all of the lights, and students volunteered to tell a ghost story while shining a flashlight on their faces from the bottom up. It gave them an eerie appearance. Some of their stories were a little scary, but most were just funny or just plain dumb.

But these stories were just a warm-up for the grand finale . . . Mr. Fry's scary story. He told us about this man who lived around the camp and everyone called him Mothman. When campers looked into the forest, they often only saw two eyes staring back at them. It seemed to look like two moths flitting about. This is why they started to call this stranger the Mothman. He had terrorized the campers for years by jumping out suddenly and chasing after them. Finally, he was caught and sent to jail. The story was creeping me out a little but not nearly as bad as it did some of the others. Some kids were whimpering or holding on to their friends real tight.

Just when I figured that the story was just about over, Mr. Fry said that the Mothman had escaped from jail that day and was seen near the camp again. With that, a big black shadow flew from the balcony of the lodge and Mr. Fry jumped up and yelled, "I'm here!"

The screaming was deafening. Some students were *scared stiff.* The lights were quickly turned on and we realized the falling shadow was just a blanket that was thrown by one of the counselors who had snuck up there during the story.

That did not bring total relief to many students who were really sobbing now. Next, Mr. Fry said that we should get our flashlights and return to our rooms. Many of the boys did not want to go outside alone and Mr. Fry and the other teachers had to escort them back to their cabins.

If the first night seemed short, this one seemed like the longest in history. There was not too much sleeping going on. And every time an acorn dropped onto the tin roof, everyone screamed. We all thought it had to be the Mothman.

Morning did finally arrive and we were all up and ready for breakfast early. The daylight made everything seem a little safer and back to normal, but many students were still talking about the Mothman.

The morning was again full of many interesting activities. We did a study of lake water creatures using microscopes. We experienced what it was like to be blind by doing a Braille hike using blindfolds and a rope. Then a local man gave a talk on snakes and he even brought several live ones along. Some of them were poisonous and others we were able to touch.

The day was going perfectly until quiet hour. Most students were too afraid to go very far from the lodge because of you-know-who . . . the Mothman. But a couple of my friends and I weren't too worried and we went back to our regular spots a little farther out in the woods. Then we made our first mistake. We decided that since we had a whole hour to spend, we would go together and look for the Marine Hike trail. We thought we knew the approximate direction, but we were way off. Once you get off the trails, everything starts looking alike. Quickly we realized that we were lost.

But being the attentive students that are, we all remembered what Mr. Fry had told us on our first day . . . "if you are lost, head downhill to the road." Well, that exactly what we did. It worked out perfectly. We reached the road and our next problem arose. Which way should we go on the road, to the right or to the left?

We all agreed that we should go to the right and that is what we did. We walked and walked but no camp was in sight. It was past an hour and quiet time was over. We figured they would be looking for us by now and they were. We decided to stay on the road and walk just a bit farther. Maybe we would see a house and could use their phone.

We walked another hundred yards and we saw an old wooden shack sitting back from the road. There appeared to be someone living there. This is where we made our next dumb move. We walked up to the house and knocked. In a few seconds a light went on and the door swung open. Standing right in front of us was Mothman! Or at least he looked like the man that Mr. Fry described in his story. We all screamed and took off as fast as we could for the road. We started running in the opposite direction of the way we had been walking. We were at a full sprint at this point. Up ahead we could see the people from our camp who were looking for us.

We were all screaming, "The Mothman, we saw the Mothman."

"Where?" Mr. Fry asked us with in a disbelieving tone.

"Down the road in that beat-up wooden shack," I panted, "we saw him there."

While some of the teachers took us back to camp, Mr. Fry and some of the counselors went down to check out our story. When they got to the shack, there wasn't anyone there. They agreed that our imaginations and fears must have gotten the best of us.

When Mr. Fry got back to camp, he came to see us. We were still a little shook up but feeling much better. We asked right away if he saw the Mothman. He told us that the Mothman story was one that he had just made up and there was never any real Mothman. I said to him that I wanted to ask just one more question, and he agreed. He then said that this would be the last one because we had to rest.

I asked Mr. Fry if there was a light on at the old wooden shack and he said, "Yes, why do you ask?"

"Oh, nothing," I said and laid down my head on the pillow. I thought to myself that I knew the Mothman was real and they weren't getting me into those woods any more.

A Tiger on the Loose

It was a busy day at the zoo. Saturdays were always busy, but this Saturday was special. The zoo had just received a new full-grown Siberian tiger from another zoo. The new addition to our local zoo has only been here for a few days and was just getting adjusted to his new surroundings. They had built a beautiful new habitat for him that looked like you were on the Siberian plains in Russia.

Today's special event at the zoo was going to be an introduction of the new tiger to the public and a talk by one of the zookeepers on Siberian tigers. Allen and I had ridden our bikes about two miles to be here for this event. The new display and show auditorium was filling up quickly and we wanted to get a seat near the front.

We all were paying close attention as the zoo handler explained about the Siberian tiger and its ways. It was very interesting, but the tiger still looked a little nervous tied to the wall with a heavy chain. The tiger sat still for a while, but eventually it must have gotten tired with the whole thing and started pulling on the chain. The zookeeper and other animal handlers didn't seem to notice anything unusual or they just weren't worried about the tiger's activities.

To our dismay, the plate holding the chain to the cement wall pulled right out and the tiger was on the loose! It ran right toward us. Why did we pick the front row? We panicked. Everyone was screaming and running in all directions, and people were bumping into each other and knocking one another down. We were lucky we weren't trampled in the stampede.

We moved along the floor to the stage area. We figured the tiger was not going to return there. He was looking for food, and we didn't want to be it. An announcement was made that all the zoo patrons were to get inside one of the animal house exhibits. We were already inside so we just stayed right where we were. The handlers had run out of the room along with everyone else before the announcement was made. We weren't sure what to do, so we stayed right where we were. The zoo was on lockdown until the loose tiger could be caged.

We felt relieved that we were relatively safe here and the tiger was on the loose outside somewhere. That was our first miscalculation. We both could not believe our eyes. We sat frozen in our spots as the giant Siberian tiger wandered back into our room.

From the talk given by the zoo handler, we knew that the tiger had a great sense of smell. He knew we were here somewhere. We were done for. What could we do? Well, I'm no acrobat or anything, but I noticed a rope that was dangling from the ceiling that probably was used when they gave exhibitions of chimps or orangutans. Could this be an avenue to safety? The tiger could never climb that rope, but could we? I quickly whispered my plan to my friend, Allen, and he agreed it was our only hope. We crept slowly toward the rope trying not to let the tiger notice us. When we were directly under the rope, Allen stood up, made a jump, and started pulling himself up to safety. So far so good . . . the tiger had not noticed us yet.

I spoke too soon. Just as I grabbed onto the rope, the tiger bounded toward me. It was roaring loudly. He was rapidly covering the ground between us and was now close enough for me to see him bare his long sharp teeth. I didn't know if I could climb fast enough to avoid his sharp claws. I knew from the talk that tigers could reach over eight feet when they stood on their hind legs and I was still only about six feet from the floor.

In my nervousness, my hands started to slip. I was sliding slowly into the clutches of a man-eating tiger. The tiger reached the rope and swung one of his flesh tearing paws at me. The only thing I could think of to do is start the rope swaying. I had to keep out of his reach. I jerked the rope in the direction away from the tiger and it moved just in time. The tiger looked angrier and hungrier.

Allen almost fell off when I jerked the rope and he yelled down to me. I just said, "Hold on tight." I figured this was my only chance. I got the rope swinging back and forth and the tiger just kept narrowly missing tearing off a piece of my flesh with his claws. Luckily for me, one of the zookeepers was passing the big window on the side of this building and saw me swinging. He figured something had to be wrong. They had not found the tiger yet, and he was going to check out this building right away. That was a big mistake on his part. He should have called for backup. When he swung the door open with a tranquilizer gun in his hand, the tiger charged right at him. Before he knew it, the tiger had knocked him down and was out the open door. The zookeeper did manage to jab the tranquilizing needle into the tiger as it passed over him. I don't know how he had the courage to do that, but at least the tiger would fall asleep in a few minutes. Well, at least Allen and I were safe for now.

In about a half hour an announcement was made that the tiger has been tranquilized and was asleep somewhere in the zoo. It also said that the animal handlers would escort all of the visitors out of the zoo. It was safe now and no one should worry.

What a relief. We had gotten much more excitement today than we were counting on.

The animal handlers took people from each building and led them to the front gate. Each handler had a tranquilizer gun just in case the tiger had awakened already. We were at the gate now and we both decided we had better go the bathroom before we got on our bikes to make the ride home. The bathroom was alongside the gate so we felt it was okay to use it.

We hurried over to the bathroom and pulled open the door. To our shock, there was the tiger and it was sitting up. We quickly pulled the door closed and leaned on it with all our might. We heard scratching and roaring, but we were holding our ground. We had the tiger trapped.

The zookeepers that were near the gate came running over when they heard us yelling for help. They told us to stand back as they slowly opened the door. They had their tranquilizer guns ready. Some of the men even had real rifles just in case.

As the door opened, we all heard a loud crash. The men swung the door open quickly and on the floor was a young boy slumped over. He did not have a scratch on him, but he was *scared stiff*. It was the boy that was scratching and banging on the door and not the tiger. He was trying to escape when we opened the door. Then the boy pointed toward the window and that's when we all realized what the crash we heard was all about. The tiger had jumped right through the glass window and was on the loose somewhere in the zoo.

I said to Allen, "Let's get out of here." I didn't have to say it again, because Allen was off toward the entrance in a flash and I was right on his heels. We had seen enough of that tiger for one day.

The Fortunetelling Machine

Sometimes when we are at the seashore during the summer, my mom and dad actually let my friends and me venture out on our own on the boardwalk. We like to do this to get away from my little sister and her friends. They are always begging Mom and Dad to go on the baby rides at the amusement pier. We do like some of the more exciting rides, but we would rather try these out on our own without my mom and dad hovering over us. They always think we take too many chances for our age and that some of the rides are definitely for older kids.

Well, this was one of those nights where we would be on our own. Our orders were to stay on the boardwalk and stay out of trouble. These two instructions sounded easy enough and we were off for some fun and adventure. One of the places we liked to hang out was the place with all sorts of virtual reality games. We loved to race each other on motorcycles, racecars, and even skis. We spent some time watching two teenage girls trying to outdo each other on a Dance Off type machine. They were really good and hardly ever missed a step. They must have spent a fortune in quarters learning how to get that good.

As we were leaving the game area, I noticed an unusual looking machine near the entrance. It was facing the boardwalk and the ocean. Written on the machine it said, "Fortunes read. Place your hand on the metal hand in front of you with your palm down. I will read your fortune for the next day. They always come true." This sounded a little goofy to me, but we went over to take a closer look.

Inside the glass-enclosed top part of the machine was a woman fortuneteller who became animated if you put in fifty cents. She would move her hand over a crystal ball that was lit up in red. At that point little lightning flashes started going off inside the ball. Then she would nod her head and out would come your fortune card into a little tray in the front of the machine. As we watched two young girls get their fortunes, they seem real excited and pleased at what they read.

We had some money left so we thought we would give it a try. Jacob went first. We watched the same eerie procedure and out came his fortune card. He told us that when the lightning appeared inside the crystal ball, he felt a little jolt in his hand that he had placed on the metal hand of the machine. This was sure some great magic fortune telling machine that someone had designed. They were making the experience as real as possible. I still didn't believe in such things, but it was fun seeing what the fortune card predicted.

We were all anxious to read Jacob's fortune card. The card was typed like it came from a printing press. How real could the predictions be if they were written hundreds of miles away by some stupid machine? But we all huddled around as Jacob read out loud, "You will have fun on the beach tomorrow with your friends." Well, this sounded like a card that could fit anyone who was dumb enough to put money in this fortunetelling rip-off.

Despite my complaining and saying this whole this was stupid, Randy quickly placed his coins into the slot and placed his hand on the protruding metal hand. The machine lit up, the lady passed her hand over the crystal ball, and lightning flashed; she nodded and out came the card. Again it was neatly done by a printing service and read, "You will enjoy riding the waves tomorrow." I was thinking again that if we didn't have a thunderstorm or something we would be riding the waves tomorrow. These predictions were lame.

Now it was my turn and I said, "I'm not going to waste my money on this nonsense."

Jacob responded with the usual, "What are you, sacred or something?"

Randy added, "Come on, we both did it and you have to try it too."

I realized that I was obligated to give up fifty cents to satisfy my friends' curiosity. So reluctantly I placed the money in the slot and my hand on the metal hand. I was slightly surprised when I felt the electric jolt in my palm as the machine operated. You did have the feeling that the machine was actually working . . . what trickery!

When the card finally appeared in the slot Jacob grabbed it up before I could reach for it. He looked astonished as he quickly handed the card to me. The card was handwritten instead of printed by a machine. This was really weird, but what I read was even worse. My card said, "Don't go in the water tomorrow or you will be hurt." My friends seemed shocked and worried as I read it to them. But I just laughed it off even though I couldn't figure out how I got a handwritten card instead of a printed one. This machine was stranger than I thought. I told the guys that I wasn't staying out of the water tomorrow just because some old card said so. But they both begged me to listen to the fortuneteller and stay on the beach only.

The next day as the families got their things together for the trek to the beach, I saw Randy talking to my father and my dad laughing. He must have felt the same way I did about the prediction card if that is what they were talking about. Anyway, I wasn't going to let some silly prediction ruin my time at the beach. I was going in the water today.

Things went well all afternoon and I had a great time swimming and riding the waves. When I heard my dad call that we were leaving the beach to go back to the house, I took one last dive and started for the shore. Just then I felt a sharp pain in my foot and by the time I got out of the water I saw that I had a good-sized cut on my foot from a seashell. My dad ran down and carried me back to a chair where my mom put a large band-aid on it. She was always prepared for anything. My friends were hovering around with that "I told you so" look on their faces. They didn't say anything though since they saw that I was in pain.

That evening we just had to revisit the fortune telling machine. It had Jacob and Randy hooked and I was feeling compelled to get a reading for tomorrow myself. When we got there, Jacob went first again and his fortune was another stupid generic one. I said to Randy that I wanted to go next to try to throw the machine off if that was possible. After all it was a machine. It couldn't think. But Randy let me go second and out came my card . . . handwritten again. What it said was even more shocking than yesterday. It read, "You can't fool me, you fool. Don't go in the water tomorrow or it could be worse."

"Worse than what?" I said out loud.

"Worse than the cut you got today, stupid. Now you must stay out of the water tomorrow!" exclaimed Jacob.

"Maybe your father will believe me now when I tell him about this latest prediction, " added Randy.

"Leave my parents out of this. I want to swim tomorrow even if the card says not to," I blurted out in a harsh tone.

We all moped around for the rest of the night on the boardwalk and eventually decided to just go back to the house. We tried to watch some TV but everyone was just bummed out about this stupid fortune telling dilemma. When my parents finally arrived back at the house my friends went to their houses for the night.

I have to admit that I had a hard time sleeping that night. I tossed and turned and mulled the situation over in my mind. How could I get the only handwritten card and why was mine the only card with a bad prediction for the next day? How could this be done? I was at a loss for an answer when I got up the next morning for breakfast. This was going to be a bummer of a day if I stayed out of the water all the time.

Down on the beach everyone was having such a good time splashing around in the water while I sat idly on the beach feeling sorry for myself. Finally, I had had enough and just ran down the beach and dove into the waves. My friends were yelling, "Don't chance it, Willie."

But it was too late. I was in and enjoying it. But that didn't last very long. Soon I was screaming bloody murder. Something was stinging my legs so bad that I thought I was going to die. I looked in the water and saw a gigantic Portuguese Man-of-War jellyfish with tentacles that looked fifty feet long. They were all around me. The stinging was intense and I was screaming bloody murder. The translucent purplish body grossed me out. I was feeling sick and felt like I was going to faint right there in the water. I felt my knees begin to buckle and I was fading fast. I was scared stiff.

All of a sudden I felt like I was floating on air. Was I in heaven already? Then I realized that my dad had scooped me up out of the water. He must have heard me scream and rushed into the water after me. He had to have seen what was stinging me, but that did not stop him. He pulled me away from the tentacles and made his way back to the beach. His legs were covered with bright red spots where he had been stung. I was sore all over, but at least I was alive.

"That's it!" said my friends in unison. "You are not going in the water tomorrow no matter what the dumb fortune teller says. I was pretty much in agreement with that idea at this point. My legs stung so bad that I could hardly stand the pain. Mom, as usual, had a temporary remedy in her bag and applied some soothing ointment to my legs and to Dad's legs as well. I knew Dad must have been in pain too, but he was not showing it outwardly. This was it. There would be no more fortuneteller predictions for me.

I was still perplexed at how this machine could produce handwritten fortune cards one time and printed ones another. And why were the handwritten ones always-bad predictions? I had to examine that machine more closely.

On the boardwalk that night, we all promised not to get our fortunes read. But you know how that can be . . . the more we tried to stay away, the more we were attracted to the dumb machine. Finally, when the stores and amusement piers were closing up for the night, we wandered back toward the fortunetelling machine and what we saw shocked us even more than the predictions.

Sneaking out of the back of the machine was a very short person. He was one of the little people we had seen a story about on TV. Now it was starting to make sense. He could see who was standing at the machine and every once in awhile he would slip in a handwritten card for a person. But why did he single out me and why did he always write me such horrible predictions? I had to find out.

As the little man closed the door in the back of the fortunetelling machine, we surrounded him. "Now we know your secret!" I growled at him. He looked scared, so I eased up on my tone of voice. "Why did you give me such bad predictions on my fortune cards?" I asked him.

The little man did not speak at first but then he uttered in a very quiet voice, "I was just trying to help you. You see, I have psychic powers and I just want to use them for good purposes. That is why I bought this fortune telling machine and spend hours inside it each day of the summer season."

If we weren't confused before, we sure were now. This small man was just trying to help me just as he had many others. He should be getting a reward for his efforts. But who would believe him, or us for that matter?

The little man spoke again as he looked straight at me and said, "I'm glad I didn't have to give you the prediction for today, because you have not been following my advice so far." And with that said, he pulled out a card from his pocket and handed it to me. The card read "Do not go into the water today or you will die." After I finished reading the card out loud for my friends, we looked around and the little man was gone. Should I believe all this crazy stuff? Should I go into the water tomorrow? After all, it is our last day at the beach. I think I'll . . . .

THE JEALOUS MAGICIAN

Do you believe in magic? I don't, but I like it just the same. It's really all just trickery, gadgets, and sleight of hand . . . but the magicians do the tricks so well that you start to believe that something really magical is happening. I have read quite a few books on magic, and I'm especially intrigued by the feats of the famous escape artist Harry Houdini. The escapes he could perform were unbelievable. He would escape from chains, locks, and trunks . . . and do all this even while underwater. Magic can be fascinating.

Most magicians will not tell how they do the tricks, but on occasion I would find one of the easier magic tricks explained in a magic book. I would work on these tricks until I was pretty good at them. My first practice test of a trick was always on my little brother. He loved the tricks and was easily fooled every time. When I got really good, I tried to do these tricks for my parents. They were a very kind audience even though I occasionally botched up a trick by dropping the hidden card or doing something else a professional magician wouldn't ever let happen.

By the way, my name is Jane and I'm in the fifth grade. I had seen real magicians perform on TV, but I was never in the actual audience while one was performing. I live in a small town of about 6,000 people and the closest a professional magician ever came to our town was a forty-five minute drive away. My parents said that the next time a magician was in our area, they would get tickets to the show and take me.

Well, now that day has come and I'm going to get to see a professional magician in person. Of course we had to bring my little brother too, but that's okay. He likes my magic tricks, so the tricks he will see today will overwhelm him.

As the show began, I find that the magic tricks were overwhelming me, too. How could he make such big things disappear and show up in another place? I sit here in awe as the magician performs one trick after another.

Of course in each magic show the magician always picks people out of the audience to act as his assistants. Everyone volunteers, but only a few people get a chance to go up on stage. When the magician announced that he was going to finish his act by doing some hypnotism on a few audience members, my hand shot up like a rocket. This is my last chance. Please pick me. And to my surprise and utter glee he does pick me.

I parade up on the stage and take a seat on one of the six chairs lined up there. Three other children and two adults sit down also. The magician or hypnotist as we call them when they are doing this part of the act, starts waving a gold watch on a long chain in front of our eyes. One of the adults and one of the children cannot be hypnotized, so they leave the stage. By now I am feeling a little drowsy and seemed to be going into a trance. The funny thing is that I can still hear the hypnotist's voice talking to the other people on stage. He is telling them to do funny things like—act like a monkey, oink like a pig, and hop around the stage like a rabbit. When it is my turn I do exactly what the hypnotist tells me to do, but I have this strange feeling that something is different with me.

When we are all finished making fools of ourselves in front of our friends and relatives, the magician wakes us up. He asks us to return to our seats and tells us that we will get a prize of a starter magic kit for participating and being good sports.

To my own surprise, I say to the magician as I am leaving the stage that I can do magic tricks, too. The next thing that happens was the real shocker. He says that he wants to see me perform one of my tricks. My mind is still feeling a bit odd so I blurt out that I can guess any card in the deck that he will hold up.

The magician chuckles, but said that we would give it a try. He shuffles the deck and holds up a card so that the audience could see what it is. He then asks me to try and guess what card he is holding.

This is too easy. I cannot see through the card, but I can see into the magician's mind. He is concentrating on the card, so I can easily determine what it is. "The two of diamonds," I say confidently.

The magician and the audience are flabbergasted.

"Right," he exclaims quite a bit surprised. He says to the audience, "Beginner's luck." Beginner's luck I think to myself, I'll show him it isn't just a lucky guess.

He holds up another card and I get that one right too. We go through a couple more and then the magician tries to trick me. For this last card he tries to think of a different card than the one he is holding up. Since I can read his mind, I just look out at the audience and read one of their minds. The audience person I'm looking at is thinking of the real card.

"Ten of clubs," I blurt out.

The magician comes over to me and whispers in my ear, "How are you doing this?"

"Just magic I guess," I reply in a low voice.

The magician leads me off the stage and says he wants to see me after the show.

When I get back to my seat, I tell my parents right away what the magician said. So when the show is over, we pick up my beginners magic kit prize and head for the magician's dressing room. As we approach, we are stopped by security. But the magician hears the commotion and comes out of his dressing room. He invites our whole family in.

He says to my parents that he would like to have me become part of his show that is going to be on national television in two weeks. Wow! It is hard for me to believe that I am actually going to be on a real TV show. I just hope this new power of reading minds will not go away before two weeks ware up.

On the way home in the car my parents ask me if the magician was somehow telling me what the cards were so I could guess them correctly. I say to them, "Ever since I was hypnotized, I can read minds if I looked straight into your eyes." They were stunned to say the least.

My dad replied, "Okay, what am I thinking now?" I tell that he was thinking of his telephone number at work. I even tell him what the number was even though I had never seen it before.

"This is utterly impossible," he blurts out, "how can this be?"

"I don't know," I respond, "but I don't like having this power. It scares me."

"Well, honey, just go on TV in two weeks and do your thing and we will have enough money from the show to send you and your brother to college," Dad reasons out loud.

I can't wait for the two weeks to pass and then I can get the TV show over with and hopefully return to normal. During these two weeks no one really wants to look me in the eye and I can't blame them. I am doing exceptionally well in school and the teacher actually asks me what I am doing differently. I don't have the heart to tell her. I actually try not to look people in the eye because I don't want to know what they are thinking. This new power can be a curse.

The magician and I practice almost every night for the show and we have everything worked out perfectly. The producers love the dress rehearsals and we are ready to go.

The night of the show I am more than a little nervous, I am *scared stiff.* But once the show starts, I overcome my stage fright and the magic act goes just great. My mom, dad, and brother are in the audience. Everyone is amazed at what I can do. I guess audience members' home addresses, number of grandchildren and even their names. People are astonished and pleased. Everyone enjoyed themselves. I am just glad it is over. I had asked the magician to do me a favor after the show and he said he would.

Back in our dressing room cameras and reporters from Entertainment Tonight, newspapers, and radio talk shows surround us. They all want to know more about what we have planned for the future. I hoped that the answer would be nothing.

When the room clears out the magician asks me what the favor is that I want him to do. I tell him that I want him to hypnotize me again. I do not tell him that being hypnotized is how I got this mind reading power, or that it is the way that I hope will get rid of it.

The magician agrees to put me under hypnosis and while he was doing it I read his mind. He is going to try to find out my secret of mind reading so he can do the show without me. He waves the gold watch in front of my eyes and I am soon under his power. This time I am really out. When I finally came to, I am sitting on my chair but the magician is nowhere to be found. My parents are staring at me but I soon realize that I can't read their minds anymore. I am cured. Maybe the magician got what he wanted, but I did too. My life can return back to normal and now I do have all the scholarship money and more. I am going to be paid handsomely for all of the interviews after the show.

Going back to school was a bit difficult. Even though I was a TV star and all, my grades start to slip back to normal. The teacher asks me again what is happening. All I could say was that magic is an unpredictable thing. Sometimes it works well and other times it can get you in trouble.

And speaking of trouble, we had not heard the last of our runaway magician. He had hypnotized himself and did gain this mind-reading power. But he had decided to use it to make money more quickly than TV. We read in the newspapers that he had been caught cheating at the casinos by reading the dealers mind. He argued that they could not prove that he was cheating and he resisted their efforts to remove him from the casino. In the struggle the magician read the workers minds and knew that they were going to hurt him soon. He broke away from them and ran out the door and right into the path of an oncoming car. Too bad he could not see into the future.

Oh, by the way, when the magician had me hypnotized the last time I lost my power to read minds, but I did gain the power to see into the future. Will this power be a curse or a blessing? We will have to wait and see. Oh, well, off to the casinos with Mom and Dad. We should do pretty well, don't you think?

THE BADLANDS

Raymond and I loved to ride our bikes. It was a good thing that we did, because our parents told us that young boys need to get exercise and that they were not going to be driving us around in the car every time we wanted to go somewhere. So far their strategy was working well. Ray and I were in pretty good physical shape and this helped us when we played sports.

Mom and Dad had some restrictions on how far we could venture from home, and also that we had to let them know where we were heading. This seemed fair enough. We knew they were just looking out for our safety.

On this blustery Saturday in early spring, Ray and I were off on an adventure to what we called 'The Badlands'. It wasn't the real Badlands like in Badlands National Park, South Dakota. It was just our Nebraska version of the badlands. The place we liked to explore had gullies, ravines, steep slopes, and other geological features of a badland. It was only a few miles from our house and we could ride on mostly back roads and dirt trails to get there.

Ray and I have been there many times before and each time we tried to find a new area to explore. On this particular day the ride took a little longer because a stiff breeze was blowing into our faces. It felt good as our summer weight coats blew out behind us as we peddled along. The breeze made it feel cooler because our "badlands" were usually very hot and extremely dry. We had water bottles along to keep ourselves hydrated. This was going to be a fun day.

"Hey, wait up!" I yelled to Ray as we approached the turnoff into the badlands area.

"Come on, Phil, do you always have to pedal like a slowpoke?" Ray yelled back. We turned onto the dusty dirt trail that headed toward the cliffs and ravines. The trail was littered with rocks so you had to be careful not to get a flat tire.

We wound our way down the trail and stopped for a rest. "Let's head down that trail towards the Mesa View Lookout," I suggested. We loved to give the places in our own little badlands their own names. We were the only ones who called them by these names, but it made it easier for Ray and me to discuss what we wanted to do.

We headed due east and peddled cautiously toward the lookout. It was a great place to look out over the canyons and you could see for miles. The going was tough because of the wind, but we were still moving along steadily. This whole area was unusual for Nebraska, which is mostly flat, but we were actually very close to Toadstool National Park, which had badlands type terrain. It was our own little world to enjoy.

As we neared the last turn to the edge of the cliff, Ray began to slow down so he would not fly off the end. We had done this many times before and knew when to go slow and when to stop. I could see Ray slowing down and I gently applied my brakes. We were on a slight slope heading downward toward the edge, so we had to make sure we didn't wait too long to brake. My brakes felt fine at first and then I got this scary feeling. My brakes didn't seem to be working anymore. I was heading toward the edge at a frightening speed.

Ray saw what seemed to be happening, and he yelled for me to jump. He couldn't grab my bike because I was going too fast. I soon realized that jumping off was the only option I had, even if it meant losing my bike over the cliff. I was *scared stiff* at this point. I could see myself falling to a painful death on the sharp rocks below.

With one last ounce of willpower, I jumped . . . but it was too late. I was already out over the end of the cliff and walking on thin air. I heard Ray scream in terror. He was going to watch his best friend fall to his death. The bike had gone one way and my body another. I could see the bike falling below me, but for some odd reason I wasn't falling nearly as fast. My summer coat was unzipped and it had billowed out like a parachute.

I soon realized that the strong winds were causing a tremendous updraft coming from the floor of the canyon. Suddenly I had this brilliant idea. I spread out my arms like a bird to catch more of the draft. It worked. Ray stood there on the cliff with his eyes wide in amazement . . . I was flying. Who could believe it? This flying thing felt great, but I knew that I would have to land somehow. I looked out over the landscape and notice a large stream about 500 yards ahead. I decided to go for it.

I looked over at the cliff and saw Ray peddling like a maniac trying to keep up with me. He followed the trail along the edge of the cliff and was now descending downward toward the stream just as I was. It seemed like the air draft was getting weaker as the hills on the sides were getting lower. It was working out perfectly for me. I did hear a small plane pass overhead and I was hoping he wouldn't get too close to me. I didn't want this landing in the stream idea to get messed up.

By now I was falling much faster than I had anticipated. I was actually in a dive like a plane would do. The water seemed to be coming at me like at an alarming rate of speed. I was beginning to worry if I would survive the impact with the water in the stream. But before I could make any adjustments . . . splash . . . I was in the stream. And to my pleasant surprise, I was still alive.

I had to fight to recover from the crash and find my bearings under the water. I looked up and saw the sunlight coming from the surface. I started to propel myself upward toward safety. I was low on breath and I was glad the stream wasn't any deeper. I was gasping for breath when I reached the surface and I felt so weak that I thought I was going to go under again at any moment.

That's when it happened. I felt something grab on to me. All I could think of was . . . a bear has me in its grasp. But I was wrong . . . it was Ray to the rescue. Luckily Ray was a strong swimmer and he pulled me back to shore. All that bike riding exercise did pay off. I just laid there panting for a few minutes before I could even talk enough to thank Ray for saving my life.

Ray said that he missed trying to save me the first time at the cliff's edge, and he wasn't going to fail a second time. It's great to have a good friend like Ray. Everyone should be that lucky.

Ray and I had to make it back home with only one bike. Mine was a total wreck at the bottom of the ravine. Ray volunteered to pedal me home on the handlebars of his bike. It wasn't a comfortable seat, but it sure beat walking.

When we finally arrived home we told my parents about the ordeal and they were very thankful that I was alive and well. My mom gave Ray a big hug and my dad shook his hand heartily. It was a happy ending to what could have been a terrible tragedy.

But just when you think it's over . . . something strange can happen to make the event even more bizarre. There was a knock at our front door and when we opened it there were several policemen. They asked to come in because they wanted to ask Ray and me a few questions. I wondered right away what we had done wrong, and I couldn't think of anything that was bad enough to get the police involved.

They said right away that we were not in any trouble, but they did say that they saw us riding back from the area of "the badlands." They wanted to know if we had seen anything unusual. Ray and I both said at once, "No, nothing out of the ordinary." We didn't want to tell them about the flying because we thought they might think we were crazy or something. Mom and Dad kept our little secret, too.

Before they left, the policeman in charge told us that someone in a small aircraft thought they saw something very unusual out in the area of the badlands earlier today. The pilot said he saw Superman flying along with his red cape flowing in the wind. Ray and I almost couldn't keep from laughing, but we didn't say a thing. The policeman said that they didn't believe the story, but the man was positive of what he had seen and his passenger saw it too . . . someone that looked like Superman was flying through the sky like a bird. "Wow!" I said, "Maybe Superman really exists after all." The cop just shrugged his shoulders and walked out the door.

When they were gone Raymond asked me if I wanted to go back to the badlands next Saturday and try it again. "Are you crazy?" I said emphatically, "flying today was a real thrill, but I think my time as Superman has come to an end."

Don't Go Near the Water

Young kids and adults seem to have this fascination for owning exotic pets. They even import some animals that are illegal to own. This does not seem to matter to them at all. They just seem to want to own something that very few other people own. Many times it is a shame for the poor animals. They may be neglected or mistreated. Then when their novelty has worn off, they are often discarded. It is the way that many of these animals are discarded that bothers me so much. If they took them to the SPCA or a pet shop it wouldn't be so bad. But more often than not, that isn't the case.

My name is Sergio and I live in the suburbs. Many times I have read in our local newspaper that wild animals have been found in people's gardens or wandering along the road. Some people even flush tropical fish down their toilet. How disgusting! There are laws against this type of treatment to animals, but they are hard to enforce. Somehow we have to do a better job of keeping these animals safe.

I am lucky that our house is on the outskirts of our development and we have access to a large track of wooded land that still contains some deer, raccoons, and other small animals. There is a nice sized pond that contains bass, sunnies, and carp to catch. It is a great place for my friends and I to play in and explore. This pond was just about perfect for us until that fateful day.

Joshua, Phil, and I were out for the day on a fishing expedition and picnic at the pond. We had done this many times before and never had trouble like we did on this day. It all started out as usual with each of us catching a few fish. We threw most of them back in because they were so small. Actually we had more fun catching the fish than anything else. We really did not want to take too many home because then we would have to clean and fillet them. That was a smelly, dirty job.

But today couldn't have been much better. The weather was perfect and we were enjoying our day out in the woods. We had placed the fish we were saving on our stringers and had them sitting in shallow water near where we were eating our lunch. It was so quiet and peaceful here. All you could hear were the birds chirping and the frogs croaking. That was until we were startled by a thrashing sound at the water's edge. We all spun around to see one of the largest crocodiles you could imagine wrestling with our stringers. He was tearing the fish to bits as he chewed them off the stringers. We were all *scared stiff.*

We weren't sure if we should just sit still and hope the beast did not notice us or run for the closest tree to climb. We decided to stay put because I heard that crocodiles could move pretty fast on land. I was hoping that the croc would have enough to eat with the fish. I was now wishing that we had kept more of them. It was too late now to worry about that . . . we had a bigger problem to worry about—much bigger!

Luckily for us the big croc had enough with the fish and slid back under the water. He disappeared as stealthily as he had arrived. These creatures were silent predators that could strike at any moment. We decided to leave our stringers in the water and get out of there while we could. We had to get home and tell our parents about what we had just witnessed. I figured that someone must have had a pet crocodile and it grew too big for their tank. They must have figured that the pond would be a good place to let it go.

We decided to stop at my house first since it was the closest. We figured that if we all told the story together our parents would believe us. We were wrong.

"What are you talking about?" Mom asked with a stern look on her face. "Are you guys seeing things?"

"No, Mom, it was a real live crocodile!" I said in my most persuasive voice.

"It was gigantic, Mrs. Rivera!" Phil blurted out with fear in his voice. "It ate all of our fish with just a few bites."

"It was savage!" belted out Josh.

Mom's last comment on the subject was, "We'll discuss this more when your father gets home." That is the statement that Mom often uses to end discussions with me because she knows I will go on and on when something is on my mind . . . and this was surely on my mind. It would be a few hours until Dad got home so we ventured over to Phil and Josh's houses to bring their moms the startling news about the pond. The reaction was about the same in both places, but Phil's mom did say that she would ask Phil's dad to walk over to the pond when he got home to check things out. Of course we wanted to go along too, and it became a family affair. Everyone went over to the pond including my nosey little sister.

While walking along the path to the pond I heard my dad say to the other men, "Maybe it was just a snapping turtle that went after the fish."

Phil's dad added, "Yeah, there is no way that there are any crocodiles around here. It must be their imaginations going wild." I knew it wasn't our imaginations. I saw the giant croc and so did the others. We would prove we were right as soon as we got to the pond.

When we all arrived at the pond, everything was peaceful and quiet just like it had always been in the past. First, our dads looked at the fishing stringers that we had left behind in our eagerness to get away from the crocodile. As they examined them, they all seemed to have funny looks on their faces. I think they all realized that it was no snapping turtle that ripped those fish to pieces. Unfortunately there still wasn't any crocodile in sight.

Our parents still made all the kids stay away from the pond as they began to slowly walk around it. My mom stayed with us. The others walked along the edge and then up the slight grade. They stood on the small cliff that overhung that one end of the pond. This was the only high point of land. The rest of the area around the pond was completely flat. The adults seemed to be staring into the water for the longest time looking for any signs of life besides the usual frogs, turtles, and snakes. From the looks on their faces, they seemed to be both pleased and disappointed. It would have been an interesting story if there was really a large croc living in this little pond.

Unfortunately, the only story that was going to be told was about three young boys with vivid imaginations. I knew right then that the boys and I had to prove that our croc story was true. We needed proof. Tomorrow we were going to return to the pond with our fishing poles and a camera.

When we arrived at the pond the next day we were shocked by what we saw. The whole pond was roped off and large signs were posted that said, "Don't Go Near The Water—Pond Temporarily Closed." Our parents must have called the police and they came down to the pond early this morning and closed it until they could prove that there was or wasn't a large crocodile living in it.

I guess our parents believed that we might have actually seen a crocodile since all three of us swore that we were not making it all up. I said to the boys,

"Let's go up on the cliff where it is safer and throw in our fishing lines. We have to solve this before the police come back." Everyone was in agreement with that idea. We wanted to solve the case but did not want to be eaten.

After we caught a few fish we were ready to lay our stringers along the shallow end of the pond where we had them the other day. If the croc was hungry, he would surely go for our bait and we would be ready with the camera to get our proof. But before we could do a thing we heard a noise coming from the pond below. In an instant, the giant croc was leaping out of the water with his jaws wide open and his long, sharp teeth frighteningly close to our legs. I never saw anything like it in my life. I didn't know crocs could jump that high out of the water.

We all quickly got over our shock and terror and moved away from the edge. We wanted to get a picture, but it was going to be from a distance. Phil said, "Give me the camera. I'll get a picture of this creature once and for all." With that said, Phil grabbed the camera and moved over to the edge to get his picture. That was a big mistake. In a split second, the croc leaped out of the water again and snapped at Phil. In his horror, Phil dropped the camera right into the pond. Now what were we going to do for proof . . . capture the croc?

I know that sounds like a crazy idea, but that is exactly what we were going to try to do. We would lay out our fish for bait and use the rope we brought to tie the croc's tail to a tree. Maybe we had watched the Croc Hunter TV show too many times, because this was an insane plan. Crocs have a powerful tail that could break your leg with one swipe. We had to be nuts to do this. Josh made the smartest suggestion of all when he said, "Let's get out of here before it's too late." Of course, Phil and I just pretended we didn't hear him speak. We were determined to prove that we had not been seeing things.

After a few minutes we had our fish in place and our rope situated so that we could sneak up on the croc while it was devouring our fish and slip the rope lariat on its tail. We already had the rope tied to a big tree. It sounded like a solid plan if only the crocodile would cooperate. We didn't have to wait long to find out the answer to that question. The croc must have smelled the fresh fish and was crawling out of the water to gobble them up. When he was comfortably eating up our day's catch, Phil and I crept around to the back of the croc and pulled the noose tightly around its tail. There was one small detail that we forgot to calculate into our plan . . . the crock could still run after us until he ran out of rope.

In a flash, the croc was on the move in a fury to get to his new prey. I was so scared I could just about run. I tripped and fell and turned to see the croc moving quickly toward me. Phil tried to drag me up, but I was dead weight. Fear had overtaken my ability to move. I could see the large jaws and teeth getting nearer to me. In a few feet I would be history.

All of a sudden the croc stopped in his tracks . . . he was at the end of the rope. The croc snapped at me and strained to break the rope. This was my opportunity to run. I had been given a second chance to live, and I was going to make the most of it. I jumped up and sprinted toward Josh and Phil. But before I could take more than a few steps I heard the rope snap and the movement of four powerful feet toward me. "Run faster!" screamed Phil. Little did he know that I was already running at my top speed. It was just that the croc was faster than me. I turned and saw the croc at my heels. My second chance at life was short-lived. I would be croc meat in a second or two.

Bang, Bang, Bang!!! It was the loudest sound I had ever heard and when I realized what had happened, it was also the most pleasant sound I had ever heard, too. There on the bank were three local policemen with rifles in their hands. Each one had put a bullet into the croc and it was lying behind me motionless. I sprinted to the safety of the policemen just in case the croc was just wounded. I knew crocs were hard to kill. Well, at least now Mom and Dad will know that we were telling the truth because we have much better proof than a picture . . . we have the real thing for them to see.

One of the policeman leaned down and asked us in a somewhat kidding voice, "Can't you boys read?" He was pointing at the "Don't Go Near The Water" sign as he was saying this. "You boys were very lucky today."

"We know, sir." I said feeling a little embarrassed. "Thanks for saving me." I knew I had been very lucky today.

The Secret of Skull Falls

Who would ever think that going over the Niagara Falls in a barrel would be an exciting thing to do . . . me, that's who. I know that going over Niagara Falls in a barrel has been done several times over the years, but I don't think I could really pull it off for several reasons. First, there are people watching the falls day and night to protect people from themselves who might actually think about trying such a stunt. Second, it is illegal. And third, my parents would have me on house arrest for a month if I lived through it.

I'm Gunther Hathaway, but my friends and family just call me Gunner. I have always been fascinated by waterfalls. Ever since the first time I saw the waterfall that is located in the woods behind our housing development, I have thought many times about what it would be like to actually go over a waterfalls. But even these falls were too high and too dangerous to attempt such a daring stunt.

Waterfalls are one of the most exciting sights I have ever experienced for many reasons. It is not just the power displayed by the rush of the water over the edge, but also the roar the water makes at it crashes into the rocks below. It is said that the explorers who came to America could hear the roar of Niagara

Falls from miles away and were confused as to what might be causing the thunderous sound. I'm sure they were as impressed as I was the first time I saw those world-famous falls.

Another thing that I enjoyed at the falls was walking behind the falling water. You put on raingear and actually get to stand behind the rushing water. It is a spectacular feeling. Of course the trip to Niagara Falls would not be complete without a ride on the Maid of the Mist. This tiny boat takes you up close to the falling water and you can feel the mist in your face. I would never want to accidentally get too close to the falls or the water would smash this tiny wooden boat to bits.

The visit to Niagara Falls made me anxious to visit out small fall back home. My friends and I love to pretend we are on an adventure, but we are also careful not to do anything too dangerous. We often visit the topside of the falls just to look over the edge and feel the power of the water falling to the pond below. The pond is pretty deep near the falls but gets much shallower the farther you get away from them. We like to fish and swim in this pond on summer days. Many times we even get close enough to the falls to feel the spray from the water crashing into the pond.

One day I called my friends Rich and Tony and asked them to meet me at the falls for a day of fishing and swimming. They were happy that I called, and we all agreed to meet at ten o'clock. I hadn't seen the waterfall since early spring and I was hoping the water in the pond would be warm enough to swim in today. When we got to the clearing that led to the pond, we all looked at the falls in amazement and trepidation. The water was coming down very slowly and the shape of a skull was exposed behind the water!

We jogged forward carrying our fishing poles, bait, and lunches. We were anxious to see what had happened to the falls and what that strange-looking rock formation was all about. Rich led the way and as we neared the pond he said, "Let's give the waterfalls a name. Let's call it 'Skull Falls' from now on." We all agreed that he had a good idea. It would help make our adventures even more exciting . . . in our own minds at least.

"Before we swim or fish, let's climb up to the top of the falls and try to find out why the water is flowing so slowly today," I suggested. We all agreed and were off making our way up the rocky slope to the top. It was a rugged climb, but we loved it. We had done it many times before, but this time we climbed like we were on a mission. We were all anxious to see what the problem was with the stream that ran over the falls. Something must be slowing it down.

We reached the top and began walking along the edge of the stream, but we did not see anything unusual except that the water level was much lower that before. We wandered a few hundred more feet and there it was . . . a beaver dam stretched across the stream with a large pool of water built up behind it. In the middle of this pool of water was a beaver lodge with a few beavers swimming around it. It was neat to see.

Even though they were interfering with the flow of the water over the falls, we decided to leave the beavers' dam intact for now. We didn't want to interfere with their family life at this time. There were probably young ones in the underwater lodge. So off we went back to the falls. The rush of the water over the falls was not nearly as exciting as usual. In fact it was just a bit more than a trickle.

As we were climbing back down to our fishing gear, I noticed that the eyes of the skull were probably being formed by the two large holes in the rocks behind the falls. "Look at those openings," I hollered to the others who were farther down the cliff. Rich and Tony turned back and stared at the opening from their viewpoint.

"I think they are little caves," shouted Tony.

"Come back up here, you guys," I yelled back, "I just noticed something. I think I have a plan. There is a ledge leading out to the openings . . . we can get to the caves."

We never saw these things before because the flow of the water usually blocked them from view. This was a special opportunity and we were going to take advantage of it. As I eyed up the ledge, I realized it was much narrower than I initially thought. Tony and Rich were a bit reluctant to venture out onto the ledge toward the cave entrance. It was wet and looked slippery. I knew I would have to lead the way if we were going to see what was inside these caves.

I placed my foot on the ledge and inched my way forward. It was about ten feet to the opening and I was going to take my time to avoid falling. It was about thirty or forty feet to the water below and I noticed that there were pieces of rock close to the bottom of the falls. I had to be careful. If the full amount of water was coming over the falls, we would never be able to cross this ledge. This was our golden opportunity.

As I moved forward, I waved for Tony and Josh to follow me. Reluctantly they stepped onto the ledge. After a few long minutes, we were all inside the first cave. We stood near the edge and looked out at the spot where we had left our fishing poles. It was a fabulous view. I was anxious to explore the cave and see if anyone had been in here before us . . . and there were.

At the back of the cave we found the remains of what looked like two spelunkers. These cave explorers must have found the cave like we did in a time when there was a gentle water flow over the falls. It appeared that they must have run into some trouble and could not escape . . . at least one of them, that is. There were two backpacks and canteens, but only one set of bones with patches of deteriorated clothing on it.

Believe it or not, the first eye of the skull connected to the other eye. It was actually all one cave. As we explored the second area we found some other interesting items. They looked like miners' tools. There were picks, hammers, and barrels filled with shiny rocks. The rocks actually looked like gold. Maybe we have struck it rich, we thought. Then a frightening thing happened . . . the falls started flowing faster.

We all rushed to the other eye of the skull cave but it was too late. The beaver dam must have given way and the water was coming over the falls as fast as ever. The ledge had virtually disappeared behind a wall of water. We were trapped. Josh and Phil started to scream at me in their panic. "I told you this was a dumb idea," shrieked Phil. Josh just stood there like he was *scared stiff.*

"We're all doomed in here," pouted Josh, "no one even knows these caves are here. They will never find us."

I knew I had to keep a clear head to think about our troublesome situation. We were trapped, and things did look dismal. I surveyed the materials that we had at our disposal and came up with one real crazy idea. You guessed it . . . the barrel. They could put me in the barrel and shove me off the end of the cave into the flowing waterfall. It was my chance to fulfill one of my dreams and it possibly was our only option for an escape. I announced my thoughts by saying, "I think I have a plan."

The boys thought that I would be killed if I tried this idiotic stunt, but I was determined to save us all since I got us into this predicament in the first place. I started emptying the biggest barrel and squeezed in. Phil and Josh reluctantly placed the wooden lid in place and asked me if I could breathe. "I'm fine," I shouted, "now let's get moving before I do run out of air."

I knew this was a long shot, but it was our only chance. In a moment I could feel myself falling and then swoosh . . . the current of the waterfall had picked me up and was carrying me downward toward the pond at a high rate of speed. Now if only the collision with the water below did not kill me we would be saved. I was hoping that the water carried me out far enough to miss the rocks. Crash!! The barrel hit the water and I could feel myself sinking. This was not exactly the experience I had envisioned when thinking about going over Niagara Falls. This was terrifying. I was just hoping that the barrel would start heading back up to the surface soon.

At last the sinking stopped and I felt the barrel start to rise. Going upward made me feel much better. When I finally reached the surface I knew I had to kick the top off the barrel so I could get out and swim to shore. I gave a mighty kick with both feet, but the lid did not budge. Maybe the lid shrank when it got wet and was now tightly sealed onto the barrel. I gave another kick with all my might. I heard a squeak. That was a good sign. I caught my breath and gave another kick . . . off popped the lid. I slid out of the barrel and looked up to where my friends were standing. They were both smiling from ear to ear. I had made it.

I quickly swam to shore and ran home to get help. Pretty soon the fire police, a rescue truck, and a fire engine were on the scene. They knew that had to slow down the water, so they first repaired the breach in the beavers' dam. Then they lowered a special rescue bucket that was hooked onto the fire truck ladder over the falls. One by one my friends were hoisted to safety. When Phil reached the side of the stream, one of the rescue team said to him, "Boy, you sure were a heavy one." Phil just smiled. We were all glad to be out of that predicament.

After we told the fire police how we got into the caves, they decided to make sure no one would ever get trapped there again. With pick axes they banged at the stone ledge until it fell into the water below. While they were doing this, all I could think about was the pile of gold we had left behind in the cave. Now it would be lost forever.

As we were walking back to my house, I said to Phil and Josh, "I sure wish we would have brought some of that gold along. We could be rich." Again Phil just smiled. When we got to my house, Phil told Josh and me that he had a big surprise for us. The next thing we knew, Phil's backpack was open and the floor was covered with gold ore. No wonder the fireman thought Phil was so heavy. We both slapped Phil on the back and said, "Great thinking under pressure, good buddy."

We planned to take the gold ore to the assay office and find out how much it was worth. The man gave us money for it in cash and then we breezed back to my house. I made the boys promise never to tell anyone where the gold came from because some day we would go back for the rest. Phil just smiled and Josh gave me that "you're out of your mind" look. I just leaned back on my chair while holding my $50,000 and said, "I think I have a plan."

The Dynamite Shack

"Let's go look at the old construction site for some wood and nails," suggested Benji.

"That's a good idea!" chimed in Alex enthusiastically.

We were all anxious to get started on our latest project of building a clubhouse behind my garage. My dad had reluctantly given the "okay" so long as we kept it back in the wooded area and away from our neighbor's property.

The construction site that we were heading toward had been abandoned for about ten years or more. The company apparently ran out of money and never finished the building. There were cinder block walls in places and piles of partly rotted lumber. There were boxes of rusty nails that we could still use for our clubhouse. We did not care about how the clubhouse looked on the outside, just as long as we had a place to hangout.

After about a fifteen-minute walk to the site we started to look around for some useful materials. We began to make a pile of wood that was still pretty solid and not rotting away. We also collected any empty soda bottles and aluminum cans that we could find so we could take them to the recycling plant to get a little extra money. We would use this money to furnish and decorate the inside of our clubhouse. We had seen some used chairs at the flea market that looked pretty comfortable.

All of a sudden we heard Benji shout, "Come over here. I've found something!" We all ran in the direction of his voice and saw him standing in front of a little shack. We had seen this shack before, but we never gone inside because it had a large padlock on the door. There was also a faded sign on the door that read "DANGER—KEEP OUT."

Benji pointed and said, "Look!" On our previous visits here we had obeyed the sign because of the lock, but now we all saw that the lock had been broken off the door and the door was slightly ajar. While the rest of us were deciding whether to enter or not, Benji was already on his way inside. This move helped us make up our minds and we decided to see what he was up to.

It was dark inside the shack so we pulled on the door a little more and it fell right off its hinges. Now we had plenty of light to see what was so dangerous about this little shack. We all rummaged through piles of papers and envelopes but there didn't seem to be anything we could use. The place was pretty messy and we decided to leave. On the way out the door, Alex noticed a wooden box tucked away in the corner. It was partly covered with trash and layers of dust.

We all crowded around the box and Alex started to brush it off. The first thing we saw was three large X's. After dusting a little more we saw the word "DANGER" again. And finally we revealed the scariest word of all . . . Dynamite. I said, "Let's get out of here and call the police."

Benji said, "What's the hurry? It's only an old dusty box."

"Don't you know what dynamite is?" I asked incredulously.

"Of course I do," Benji replied in an agitated tone. "But I have never seen a real box of it before. I want to open the box and feel a real piece of dynamite. We can pretend we are in the old West and going to blow up a bridge or something."

"Are you crazy? I replied honestly.

Alex just laughed and said, "Let's get out of here before something bad happens." I was surely in agreement with that thought.

Before we could get out the door, Benji had opened the box and was handling a stick of the dynamite. He must not have realized the potential of even just one stick of this stuff.

I tried to explain to Benji that Alfred Nobel had invented this explosive for peaceful uses, but it soon was being used to destroy all kinds of things. That is why he wanted his profits from the invention of dynamite to go toward funding the Nobel Peace Prize and other prizes for discovery, the arts, and inventions. Benji was not too interested in the history of dynamite; he was mainly interested in holding a piece of it.

Finally we talked Benji into leaving the shack and to heading home with our lumber and nails. As we walked along, Benji seemed a bit distant and nervous, too. We thought he was just angry with us for not letting him play with the dynamite any more. We knew he would get over it and be thankful that we were just trying to keep him safe.

When we arrived at my house, we dropped off the materials in the woods behind my garage and headed into my house to tell my mom what we found. Benji said that he was heading home for lunch and that he would see us later. Mom suggested we call the local police right away so they could secure the site where the dynamite was located until it could be safely taken away.

In a matter of minutes the police were at our doorstep and they asked Alex and me to lead them to the dynamite shack. We rode along in the police car to the construction site and pointed out the shack. They said that we should stay by the car and that they would check things out.

The two policemen entered the shack and found the box right where we said it was. But in a flash they were standing outside the entrance to the little building and yelling something to us. We started to move toward them, but they gestured to stay back. They both jogged toward us and one of the men said, "There are two sticks of dynamite missing from the box. Did you boys take any?"

Alex and I both exclaimed, "Oh, no, so that's why Benji looked so suspicious as we walked home. Benji must have taken the two sticks of dynamite to his house. I sure hope he doesn't try to light . . ."

KA-BOOM!!! We heard the loudest blast imaginable coming from the direction of Benji's house. The policeman said, "Get in the car and show us where Benji lives!" He put on the flashing lights and siren, and we were off at breakneck speed toward Benji's. I was only hoping that it was something else that exploded, but in my heart I knew it was Benji.

We sped around corners at top speed and Alex and I were thrown around the back seat even though we had our seat belts on securely. When we got to Benji's street, we did not have to tell the police where his house was because there was a cloud of smoke coming from behind his house. I started to feel sick to my stomach.

We came to a screeching halt right in front of Benji's place, and we all jumped out. The police told us to stay at the car, but we were not listening to them this time. As soon as they were out of view behind the house, we took off around the other side of the house. When we got to the backyard we were horrified. The two-car garage was blown apart. Some of the cinder block walls were still standing, but the back wall had collapsed and the roof was on fire. Benji's mom was screaming and the police were trying to get the pile of cinder blocks off of Benji. We saw his arm sticking out of the rubble, but it looked lifeless. Now I was *scared stiff*.

In a matter of moments, the fire company and rescue squad were at the scene, and Benji was removed from the pile of cinder blocks. He looked bad, but he was still breathing. Benji was trying to say something to the police, but they were having a hard time understanding him.

I Love Scary Stories

I hate Mondays and today starts another week of school. The reason I don't like school so much is that I have trouble reading and writing. I wish I could get better, but my family moves around so much that I keep missing important things that I should know. As soon as I get settled in and start to feel a little comfortable . . . we move again. By now I have just given up on learning and I just keep to myself. The teachers try to work with me, but I just don't care much anymore. It's hopeless.

"Donyell, time to get your breakfast!" yelled my mother up the steps to my bedroom. "Hurry up. I was late for work twice last week because of your slowpoke antics. You have to go to school and that's that."

Why should I hurry to get to a place where all I feel is that I'm a failure? Why should this Monday be any different than the others?

Boy, was I wrong. Instead of Mrs. Brown our usual teacher, meeting us at the doorway . . . it was a man. And he was a tall man at that. I'm tall, so that gave us something in common right away. I want to be a professional basketball player some day. They make lots of money and many of them get into college even if they have bad grades like me. I'm pretty good at basketball already, and I know I can be a pro if I work hard at it.

"Hi, everyone, I'm Mr. Williams. I will be your substitute for the day. Your teacher is at a conference and will be back tomorrow. But for today, I want us to have fun and also learn as much as we can together."

I liked hearing the fun part, but I didn't like the learning part because that meant reading, writing, and other things that I wasn't good at. If I could just sit here all day and say or do nothing, that would be fine with me. In fact, that's what I do most days anyway. Why should I change for a substitute that will be here today and gone tomorrow . . . just like me and this school. Who knows when we will be packing up to leave for the next place?

"Since I do not know all of you and you don't know me, I want to take this opportunity to allow each of you to ask me one question," stated Mr. Williams.

Everyone was excited to ask him about his favorite car, favorite sports team, did he have any pets, favorite vacation spot and all kinds of other junk. I sat near the back, so I had a long time to think about my question. When it got to be my turn, I asked Mr. Williams if he ever thought about being a professional basketball player, since he was so tall.

I was surprised when Mr. Williams said, "Good question." Most times in school, this was not the response I received for one of my questions. Actually I stopped asking very many questions the last couple of years. What was the use? I was still lost most of the time. Even when they answered it, I still had another question or two . . . but it was no use. "Donyell, I was almost a professional basketball player. I played on several semi-professional teams after I graduated from college."

I raised my hand with another question and this time I got lucky and he let me ask it. "Did you actually graduate from college instead of just turning pro after a year or two?"

Mr. Williams's answer surprised me. He smiled and said, "I didn't go to college to play basketball and become a pro. I went to college to get a good education because I know that the chances of making the NBA are about one in a million."

"But, weren't you pretty good?" I blurted out not being able to contain myself.

"Sure, I made the all-conference team, set several school records, and was voted the most outstanding senior athlete. But I was still just a small fish in a big sea. There were thousands of players around the country that were much better than I was. It was off to finding a teaching job for me. And I'm really glad I became a teacher. It's a great job. Thanks, everyone for your questions and now we have to get started on our social studies lesson about which explorers claimed land in the New World and where this land is located."

So now it begins all over, I thought to myself. Another boring lesson that I won't understand or enjoy, something to read in the book, and then something to write. I'm doomed again! But another surprise, this lesson was actually getting my attention, and Mr. Williams even asked me a question that I just happened to know the answer to. I started to raise my head up a little more and look at the pieces of colored paper he was placing on the map. This wasn't so bad after all. I was getting the idea and things were starting to make sense. It was a nice feeling actually.

But that came to a quick halt when I heard Mr. Williams say these frightening words, "Now we are going to have language arts class."

And just when things were going so well I thought. What would I have to do now? Mr. Williams told us to come up and sit on the rug. That wouldn't be too bad because at least I wouldn't have to read or write anything, *yet*. Mr. Williams sat in the teacher's chair and said that we were going to learn about what it takes to become a professional writer. He said that we were all amateur writers already. Apparently, he had not heard about me yet. He told us about how he had written several books and what it took to get them published. It sounded like a lot of work to me. He said he worked for two years on one book. I can't work for two minutes on writing something without a breakdown.

The thing that got my attention the most was when he told us that he was currently writing a book for children that were about our age and that he was going to tell two of the stories in the book. The first one was entitled *The Substitute* and the other was called *The Baby Shark*. They were both a bit scary, but I loved them. When he was finished with the second story, the whole class asked him to tell another one. But we didn't have time. We had to go to lunch now. As we were getting up to go back to our seats, I took a chance and told Mr. Williams that I like those kinds of stories and that I would like to read his book of them.

To my great surprise, Mr. Williams said, "I will send a copy of my stories to your teacher, but . . . ." I knew it, there was always a but or two in school and at home . . ."I want you to write a scary story for me after lunch."

I knew it; I'm really doomed now. I never could think of anything to write about and even if I could, I had a hard time putting it down on paper correctly.

Mr. Williams announced that at lunch we should think about some ideas for writing a scary story. He told us to use some of our personal experiences mixed with imagination and exaggeration. I might as well go home now. I'll never get an idea for a story by this afternoon. Then Mr. Williams said, "You have to look at things from a different viewpoint . . . through a writer's eye."

What did that mean? I thought to myself. Oh, well, off to lunch. What are we having today? I never look at the menu. I just buy whatever they have every day. Mom doesn't have time to pack a lunch for me. Oh, no. Today we are having what everybody calls "mystery meat." The lady behind the serving counter always seems to have a sneer on her face as she piles these lumps of foul tasting, disgusting looking pieces of meat on our plates. Does she know something we don't know? BANG! I almost dropped my tray. Everyone turned to look at me but I didn't care. I had an idea for a story. Maybe that "writer's eye" thing does work.

When we got back to class, we had math. I could hardly pay attention, but that was nothing new. I had this story rolling around in my mind and I couldn't wait to get it out. I knew the writing part would be hard, but I thought it was worth giving it a try because I love scary stories.

After math was over, Mr. Williams announced that we were going to start our scary stories. He had written our game plan on the board. First, we would organize our ideas in an outline form with characters, setting, plot, problem, solution, and ending. We only needed to write a few words for each section. I could handle that.

The next step was that we were going to the computer lab to write our stories on the computer. He told us to just let our ideas flow and that we could go back and make corrections later. He reminded us to save our work all the time so we wouldn't suddenly lose it all.

I was anxious to get started. I had my ideas and the computer would help me write it. Mr. Williams said that this is how most professional writers work. I can't believe it; I'm actually excited about writing something.

My story was titled "Mystery Meat" and I had characters from our class in it including myself. The setting was easy because it was something that I saw every day. The plot was the tricky part. I knew how I wanted it to end, but how was I going to get to that point and have my story be a bit scary? I worked hard for a full forty-five minutes and at last I was done with that part. It sounded pretty good if I do say so myself. Now I had fifteen minutes to use the computer's spelling and grammar checker on my story. Mr. Williams also told me to read it over a few times to make sure all parts of it made sense and that the spell or grammar checker didn't miss anything. Luckily, I did that because the computer did miss a few things.

Now I was ready for the next step . . . the presentation to the class. Usually, I really hated this part and was *scared stiff* to speak in front of the class. Many times I said I was just not ready or I forgot my paper. Not this time. I wanted to be first if I could.

Everyone was shocked when I volunteered to be the first author to read. I could hardly believe it myself that I was a real author this time!

I started to read my story and noticed everyone seemed interested as soon as I read my title . . . *Mystery Meat*. I knew I wasn't so good at reading either, but since I wrote this story, I knew all the words. I had also read it over so many times before that the words seemed to just flow out.

I was excited about the scary parts and I made my voice sound a little scary, too. When I told them how the cafeteria lady went around and found dead animals on the road, chopped them up, and mixed them with bacon fat to make the "mystery meat" . . . everyone went, "yu-uck!" I said that if she couldn't find road kill, she would drive around at night and try to steal people's pets. I ended by saying that if they ever see someone near their house carrying a kitchen knife and wearing a cafeteria worker's uniform, "lock your doors and hide your pets because they may be tomorrow's 'mystery meat' at lunch."

I knew instantly by the looks on their faces that my story was a success. And when they all clapped without the teacher telling them to, I knew that my story was a hit. Maybe I could be a real author some day. Maybe Mr. Williams has a point about college and not making it to the NBA. Maybe I could try as hard in school as I do at basketball practice. My coach always says it is all about "attitude." Well, Mr. Williams should be a coach too, because he sure changed *my* attitude about a lot of things today. Wait till Mrs. Brown sees the new me! I think Mom and Dad will like the changes, too.

Breinigsville, PA USA
14 January 2010
230727BV00001B/2/P